A GAME WITH
ONE WINNER

A GAME WITH ONE WINNER

BY

LYNN RAYE HARRIS

First published in Great Britain 2013
by Mills & Boon, an imprint of Harlequin (UK) Limited.
Large Print edition 2013
Harlequin (UK) Limited, Eton House,
18-24 Paradise Road, Richmond, Surrey TW9 1SR

© Lynn Raye Harris 2013

ISBN: 978 0 263 23212 7

Harlequin (UK) policy is to use papers that are natural,
renewable and recyclable products and made from
wood grown in sustainable forests. The logging and
manufacturing process conform to the legal environmental
regulations of the country of origin.

Printed and bound in Great Britain
by CPI Antony Rowe, Chippenham, Wiltshire

For MPP

CHAPTER ONE

Russian Billionaire Rumored to Be Acquiring Troubled Department Store Chain

SHE WAS HERE. Roman Kazarov knew it as surely as he knew his own name, though he had not yet seen her. The woman at his side made a noise of frustration, a tiny little sound meant to draw his attention back to her. He flicked his gaze over her, and then away again.

Bored. The woman was beautiful, but he was bored. One night in her bed, and he was ready to move on.

Her fingers curled possessively around his arm. He resisted the urge to shake them off. He'd brought her here tonight on impulse. Because Caroline Sullivan-Wells would be here. Not that Caroline would care if he had a woman on his arm. No, she'd made it very clear five years ago that she didn't care about him in the least.

Had never cared.

Once, her rejection had cut him to the bone. Now, he felt nothing. Nothing but cold determination. He'd returned to New York a far different man than he'd left it five years ago.

A rich man. A ruthless man.

A man with a single goal.

Before the month was out, he would own Sullivan's, the luxury chain of department stores founded by her family. It was the culmination of everything he'd worked so hard for, the symbolic cherry on top of the ice-cream sundae. He did not need Sullivan's, but he wanted it. Once, he'd been an acolyte at the feet of Frank Sullivan. And then he'd been unceremoniously tossed out, his work visa terminated, his dreams of providing a better life for his family back home in Russia shattered.

All he'd dared to do was fall in love with Caroline, but that one act had been the same as strapping on wings made of wax and flying too close to the sun. He'd fallen far and fast.

But now he was back. And there was nothing Caroline or her father could do about what he'd set in motion.

As if in answer to some hidden command, the

crowd parted to reveal a woman standing on the other side of the room. She was deep in conversation. The glow from the Waterford chandelier overhead shone down in just such a way that it appeared to single her out, wreathing her golden-blond head and milky skin in a nimbus of pale light.

Roman's gut clenched. She was still beautiful, still ethereal. And she still affected him, which only served to anger him further. He had not expected it, this jolt of remembered lust and bittersweet joy. He stood there and willed the feeling away until he could look at her coldly, critically.

Yes, much better. That was what he wanted to feel—disgust. Hatred.

His jaw tightened. She chose that moment to look up, almost as if she'd sensed something was wrong, as if there was a disturbance in her well-ordered circle of friends. There was a crease in the smooth skin over her hazel eyes, as if she was annoyed at being interrupted.

But then she saw him. Her eyes widened, her pink lips dropping open. She put a hand to her chest, then thought better of it and dropped it to her side—but not before he saw how he affected her. For a long moment, neither of them looked away. She broke the contact first, saying something to the person she'd been talking to, before she turned and fled through a door behind her.

Roman stiffened. He should feel triumphant, yet he strangely felt as if she'd rejected him again. As if his world were about to come crashing down just as it had five years ago. But that was not possible, not any longer. *He* had the upper hand now. He was the victor, the conqueror.

And yet bitterness coiled inside him, twisting and writhing on the floor of his soul, reminding him of how far he'd fallen, and how hard. Reminding him of how much that fall had cost him before he'd been able to pull himself up again.

"Darling," the woman at his side said, drawing his attention from the door through which Caroline had disappeared, "can you fetch me a drink?"

Roman gazed down at her. She was pretty, spoiled, an actress with a face and body that usually drove men wild. She was used to commanding attention, to having her whims obeyed without question.

But what she saw in his face must have given her pause. She took a step back, her fingers sliding over the sleek fabric of his bespoke tuxedo. She was already calculating, already trying to recover from her mistake.

Too late.

"I do not fetch," he told her coolly. And then he reached into his breast pocket and pulled out his wallet. He took out five crisp one-hundred-dollar bills and pressed them into her hand. "Enjoy yourself for as long as you wish. When you are finished, take a cab home."

She reached for him as he turned. "You're leaving me?"

Her eyes were wide, her confidence in her beauty shaken. He would have felt sorry for her, except that he was certain loads of interested men would swarm around her as soon as he walked away. Roman took her hand from his sleeve, lifted it to his lips and pressed a kiss to the back of it. "It is not meant to be, *maya krasavitsa*. You will find another who deserves you."

And then he left her standing alone as he went in search of another woman. A woman who would not escape him this time.

Caroline took the elevator down to the first floor and hurried out to the sidewalk. Her heart hammered in her head, her throat, and she clutched her wrap to her body and tried to breathe evenly. *Roman.*

She blinked back the sudden tears that hovered, and gave the doorman a shaky smile when he asked if she'd like a taxi.

"Yes, please," she said, her voice a touch breathless from her flight. Of all the people to be in that room tonight. And yet she should have expected him, shouldn't she? She'd read that he was back in town. The newspapers couldn't seem to leave the subject of Roman Kazarov alone. Or his mission.

Caroline's fingers tightened on the silk wrap. It would be hopelessly wrinkled when she was done, but she hardly cared. She'd known she would have to see him again, but she hadn't expected it to happen quite yet. No, she'd expected to face him in a boardroom—and even that thought had been almost enough to make her lose her lunch at the time.

How could she face him again? How? One moment, one look from across the room, and she was a jittery wreck of raw emotion. He had always had that effect on her, but she was nevertheless stunned that he still did. After all this time. After everything.

"Caroline."

Her spine melted under the silken caress of her name on those lips she'd once loved so much. Once, but no more. She was a woman now, a woman who had made her choice. She'd do the same thing again, given the circumstances. She'd saved Sullivan's then; she would save it now, too.

No matter that Roman Kazarov and his multinational conglomerate had other ideas.

She turned with a smile on her lips. A smile that shook at the corners. She only hoped it was too dark for him to notice.

"Mr. Kazarov," she said, her voice a little too shrill, a little too brittle.

She needed to find her strength, her center—but she was off balance, her system still in shock from the surprise of seeing him in that room tonight.

Her heart took a slow tumble over the edge of the shelf on which it sat, falling into her belly, her toes. She felt hollow inside, so hollow, as she gazed up into those bright, ice-blue eyes of his. He was still incredibly handsome. Tall, broad-shouldered, with dark hair and the kind of chiseled features that made artists itch to pick up their palette knives and brushes.

Or made photographers snap-happy. Yes, she'd seen the photos of him since he'd burst onto the scene a little over two years ago. She still remembered the first time, when Jon had handed her the paper over breakfast and told her she needed to see who was featured there.

She'd nearly choked on her coffee. Her husband had reached for her hand and squeezed it. He was the only one who knew how devastating news of Roman would be to her. In the years that followed, she'd watched Roman's rise with trepidation, knowing in her gut that he would return one day.

Knowing that he would come for her.

Roman tsked. "After all we were to each other, Caroline? Is this how you greet an old friend?"

"I wasn't aware we were friends," she said, remembering with a pang the way he'd looked at her that night when she'd informed him they couldn't see each other anymore. He'd just told her he loved her. She'd wanted to say the same words back to him, but it had been impossible. So she'd lied. And he'd looked…stunned. Wounded. And then he'd looked angry.

Now, he looked as if he could care less. It disconcerted her. She was off balance, a mess inside. A churning, sick mess, and he looked cool, controlled. Calm.

But why was she a mess? She'd done what she'd had to do. She would do it again. She tilted her chin up. Yes, she'd done the right thing, no matter the personal cost. Two people's happiness had been nothing compared to the well-being of the countless people whose livelihoods had depended upon Sullivan's.

Roman shrugged. "Then we are certainly old acquaintances." One eyebrow arched as his gaze slid down to where she clutched the wrap over her breasts. She'd worn a strapless black dress tonight, but she felt as if she were naked under the silk, the way his eyes took their time perusing her. Heat flared in her core. Unwelcome heat. "Old *lovers*," Roman said, as his eyes met hers again.

She turned and stared across Fifth Avenue toward the park, her insides trembling. Traffic was jammed up, barely moving due to some unseen obstruction, and she knew her cab would be a long time in arriving. How would she endure this?

She'd hoped beyond hope that she would never see him again. It would be easier that way. Safer.

"You do not wish to be reminded?" Roman asked. "Or have you decided to pretend it never happened?"

"I know what happened." She would never forget. How could she when she had a daily reminder of the passion she'd once shared with this man? Panic threatened to claw its way into her throat at the thought, but she refused to let it. "But it was a long time ago."

"I was sorry to hear about your husband," he said then, and her stomach twisted into a painful knot.

Poor Jon. Poor, poor Jon. If anyone had deserved happiness, it had been him. "Thank you," she said, the lump in her throat making her words come out tight. Jon had been gone for over a year now, but it still had the power to slice into her when she thought of those last helpless months when the leukemia had ravaged his body. It was so unfair.

She dipped her head a moment, surreptitiously dashing away the tears threatening to spill down her cheeks. Jon had been her best friend in the world, her partner, and she missed him still. Thinking of Jon reminded her that she had to be as strong as he'd been when facing his illness.

Roman was a man, and men could be defeated. "It won't work," she said, her voice fiercer than she'd thought she could manage at that moment.

Roman cocked an eyebrow. So smooth. "What won't work, darling?"

A shiver chased down her spine. Once, he'd meant the endearment, and she'd loved the way his Russian accent slid across the words as he spoke. It was a caress before the caress. Now, however, he did it to torment her. The words were not a caress so much as a threat.

She turned and faced him head-on, tilting her head back to look him in the eye. He stood with his hands in his pockets, one corner of his beautiful mouth slanted up in a mocking grin.

Evil, heartless bastard. That was what he was now. What she had to think of him as. He wasn't here to do her any favors. He would not be merciful.

Especially if he discovered her secret.

"You won't soften me up, Roman," she said. "I know what you want and I plan to fight you."

He laughed. "I welcome it. Because you will not win. Not this time." His eyes narrowed as he studied her. "Funny, I would have never thought your father would step down and leave you in charge. I always thought they would carry him from his office someday."

A shard of cold fear dug into her belly, as it always did when someone mentioned her father these days. "People change," she said coolly.

And sometimes those changes were completely unexpected. A wave of love and sadness filled her at the thought of her father, sitting in his overstuffed chair by the window and staring at the lake beyond. Some days he recognized her. Most days he did not.

"In my experience they don't. Whatever was there at the start will continue to be there in the end." His gaze slid over her again, and her skin prickled. "People sometimes want you to think they've changed, in order to protect themselves, but I find it's never true."

"Then you must not know many people," she said. "We all change. No one stays the same."

"No, we don't. But whatever the essence was,

that remains. If one is heartless, for instance, one doesn't suddenly grow a heart."

Caroline's skin glowed with heat. She knew he was speaking of her, speaking of that night when she'd thrown his love back in his face. She wanted to deny it, wanted to tell him the truth, but what good would it do? None whatsoever.

"Sometimes things are not as they seem," she said. "Appearances can be deceptive."

As soon as she said it, she knew it was the wrong thing to say. His icy eyes grew even frostier as he studied her. "I have no doubt you would know this."

Fury and sadness warred inside her. The only thing to do was to pretend not to understand his meaning. Caroline gave a superior sniff. "Nevertheless, Daddy has reevaluated his priorities. He's enjoying himself at his country estate these days. He worked hard for it, and he deserves it."

There was a lump in her throat. She gritted her teeth and turned to look hopefully for a taxi, willing herself not to cry as she did so. She wasn't ordinarily overcome with emotion, but thinking about her father's illness in the presence of this man she'd once loved was a bit overwhelming.

"I had no idea you were interested in taking over the business someday," Roman said, his tone more than a bit mocking. "I'd rather thought your interests lay elsewhere."

She whipped around to look at him. "Such as shopping and getting my nails done? That was never my plan."

It had been her parents' plan, however. It was simply not done for a Sullivan woman to work. They married well and spent their days doing charitable work, not dirtying their hands in the business. No matter that she'd wanted to learn the business, or that her father had indulged her a bit and let her intern there—because business experience would do her good in her charitable duties, he'd said over her mother's protests. Jon had always been the one intended to run the department store chain once her father retired.

Which Frank Sullivan would not have done anytime in the next twenty years had the choice not been taken from him. Now that Jon was dead, there was no one else but her. And she was good at what she did, damn it. She had to be.

"You've had a bad year," Roman said softly, and her heart clenched. Yes, she'd had a bad year. But she still had Sullivan's. More importantly, she had her son. And for him, she would do anything. Sullivan's would be his one day. She would make sure of it.

"It could always be worse," she said, not meeting Roman's hard gaze. She'd told herself repeatedly that things could always be worse just so she could get through the day—but she really didn't want to know how much worse. Losing a husband to cancer and a father to dementia was pretty damn bad in her book.

"It *is* worse," he said. "I'm here. I don't arrive on the scene until a company is struggling, Caroline. Until profits are squeezed tight and every month is a struggle to pay your suppliers just enough so they'll keep the shipments coming."

Caroline blinked. *The stores.* Of course he was talking about the stores. For a minute, she'd thought he was being sympathetic. But why would he be? She was the last person he'd ever show any compassion for.

And she could hardly blame him, could she? They hadn't exactly parted on the best of terms.

Though her heart ached, she feigned a laugh that was as light as the evening breeze. It tinkled gaily, as if she hadn't a care in the world, when in fact she felt the weight of her cares like an anvil yoked to her neck.

"Oh Roman, really. You've done quite well for yourself, but your information cannot always be correct. This time, you are wrong. Dead wrong. You won't get Sullivan's, no matter how you try." She waved a hand toward Fifth Avenue, encompassing the park, the horse-drawn carriage with its load of tourists passing by, and the logjam of cars and trucks packing the avenue. "Times have been bad everywhere, but look around you. This city is alive. These people are working, and they need the kind of goods Sullivan's provides. They want what we have. Our sales are up twenty percent this quarter. And it will only get better."

She *had* to believe that. Her father had made some bad decisions before anyone realized he was ill, and she was working her hardest to fix them. It wasn't easy, and she wasn't assured of success, but she wasn't ready to give up yet, either.

Roman smirked. Literally smirked. "Twenty percent in *one* store, Caroline. The majority of your stores are suffering. You should have sold off some of the less profitable branches, but you didn't. And now you are hurting."

He took a step toward her, closed the space between them until she could feel his heat. His power. She wanted to take a step back, to put distance between them, but she would not. She would never give an inch of ground to this man. She couldn't. She'd made her choice five years ago and she would stick by the rightness of it until the day she died.

"Thank you for your opinion, as unsolicited as it might have been," Caroline said tightly. The nerve of the man! Of course she'd thought of selling off a few of the stores, but when she'd tried, the offers hadn't exactly been forthcoming. It should have been done two years ago, but she hadn't been the one in charge then. By the time she'd taken the lead, the economy had tanked and no one wanted to buy a department store. She was doing the best she could with the resources she had.

"I've done my research," Roman said. "And I know the end is near for Sullivan's. If you wish to see it continue, you'll cooperate with me."

Caroline tilted her chin up again. She'd been strong for so long that it was as natural to her as breathing. She might have been young and naive five years ago, when she'd loved this man beyond the dictates of reason or sense, but no longer.

"Why on earth would I do that? Are you saying I should just trust you? Sign over Sullivan's and trust that you'll 'save' the stores that have been in my family for five generations?" She shook her head. "I'd be a fool if I did business that way. And I assure you I am no fool."

Miraculously, a taxi broke through the traffic and pulled to the curb then. The uniformed door-man drew open the door with a flourish. "Madam, your taxi."

Caroline turned without waiting for an answer and entered the cab. She was just about to tell the driver where to take her when Roman filled the frame of the open door.

"This is my taxi," she blurted as he shifted her over with a nudge of his hip.

"I'm going in the same direction." He settled in beside her and gave the driver an address in the financial district. Caroline wanted to splutter in outrage, but she forced herself to breathe evenly, calmly. Her heart was a trapped butterfly in her chest. She couldn't lead Roman to her door. She couldn't bear to have him know where she lived. If Ryan came outside for some reason…

No. Caroline gave the driver the address of a town house in Greenwich Village. It wasn't *her* town house, but she could walk the two streets over to her own house once the cab was gone.

"How did you know we were going in the same direction?" she demanded as the taxi began to inch back into traffic.

He shrugged. "Because I'm in no hurry. Even if you went north, I could eventually go south again."

Caroline tucked her wrap over one shoulder. "That seems like a terrible waste of time."

"I hardly think so. I have you alone now."

Her heart thumped. Once, she would have been giddy to be alone with him for a long cab ride. She would have turned into his arms and tilted her head back for his kiss. Unwelcome heat bloomed in her cheeks, her belly. How many clandestine kisses had they shared in taxis such as this one?

Caroline didn't want to think about it. She slid as far away from him as she could get, and turned to stare out the window at the mass of humanity moving along the sidewalks. A young woman in a yellow dress caught her eye as she walked beneath a streetlamp, her arm looped into the man's beside her. When she threw her head back and laughed, Caroline felt a pang of envy. When was the last time she'd laughed so spontaneously?

Arrested by her laugh or her beauty, or some unidentifiable thing Caroline couldn't see, the man drew the girl into his arms. Caroline craned her neck as the taxi moved past, watched as the girl wrapped her arms around the man's neck and their lips met.

When she turned back, she could feel Roman's eyes on her in the darkened taxi.

"Ah, romance," he said, the words dripping with cynicism.

Caroline closed her eyes and swallowed. She bit her lip against the urge to say she was sorry for any pain she'd caused him. They'd said everything five years ago. It was too late now, and she wasn't the same person she'd been then.

"What do you want from me, Roman?" Her voice sounded strained to her own ears. If he noticed, he didn't comment.

"You know what I want. What I came here for."

She turned to look at him, and barely stopped herself from sucking in her breath at the sight of him all dark and moody beside her. After five years, was she still supposed to be this affected by his dark male beauty?

"You're wasting your time. Sullivan's isn't for sale at any price."

There was silence between them for a long moment. And then he burst into laughter. His voice was rich, deep and sexy, and a curl of heat wound through her at the sound.

"You will sell, Caroline. You will do it because you can't bear to see it cease to exist. Be stubborn—and watch when your suppliers cut off your line of credit, one by one. Watch as you have to close one store, and then another, and still you cannot fill your orders or keep your stores supplied with goods. Sullivan's is known for quality, for luxury. Will you cease to order the best, and settle for second best? Will you tell your customers they can no longer have the Russian caviar, the finest smoked salmon, the specialty cakes from Josette's, the designer handbags from Italy or the custom suits in the men's haberdashery?"

A shiver traveled up her spine, vibrated across her shoulder blades. Her stomach clenched hard. Yes, it was that bad. Yes, she'd been studying the list of her suppliers and wondering how she could cut corners and still keep the quality for which Sullivan's was known. The specialty food shop was hugely expensive—and yes, she'd thought of downsizing that department, of eliminating it in some markets.

She'd wanted to ask her father. She'd wanted to sit at his feet and ask him what he thought, just as she'd wanted to turn to Jon and ask him for his opinion. But they were unavailable, and she would not choke. She would make the hard choices. For Ryan. She would do it for Ryan.

Family was everything. It was all she had.

"I won't discuss this with you, Roman," she said, her voice as hard as she could make it. "You don't own Sullivan's yet. If I have anything to say about it, you won't ever get that chance."

"This is the thing you fail to understand, *solnyshko*. You have no say. It is as inevitable as a sunset."

"Nothing is inevitable. Not while I have my wits. I intend to fight you with everything I have. You will not win."

His smile was lethally cold. And dangerously

attractive if the spike in her temperature was any indication.

"Ah, but I will. This time, Caroline, I get *my* way."

Her heart thumped. "And what's that supposed to mean? Surely you aren't still brooding over our brief affair. You can't mean to acquire Sullivan's simply to get revenge for past slights."

She said the words as if they were nothing, as if the mere idea were ridiculous, though her pulse skittered wildly in her wrists, her throat.

The corners of his mouth tightened, and her insides squeezed into a tight ball.

"Brooding? Hardly that, my dear. I've realized since that night that my…" he paused "…*feelings*… were not quite what I thought they were." His gaze dropped over her body, back up again. "I was enamored with you, this is true. But love? No."

It should not hurt to hear him say such a thing, but it did. She'd loved him so much, and she'd believed that he had loved her in return.

And now he was telling her he never had. That it was all an illusion. The knowledge hurt far more than she'd have thought possible five years after the fact.

"Then why are you here?" she asked tightly. "Why does Sullivan's matter to you? You own far more impressive department stores. You don't need mine."

His laugh was soft, mocking. "No, I don't need them." He leaned toward her suddenly, his eyes gleaming in the light from the traffic. Her stomach clenched in reaction, though she hardly knew what she was reacting to.

"I *want* them," he growled. "And I want *you*."

CHAPTER TWO

Kazarov Ruthless in Business and Bed,
Beauty Says

HE HADN'T INTENDED to go that far, but now that he had, it was interesting to watch her reaction. Her breath hitched in sharply, her hazel-green eyes widening. She dropped her lashes, shielding her eyes from his as she worked to control her expression.

Since the moment she'd spun toward him on the pavement, he'd been remembering what it had been like with her. It annoyed him greatly. He had his pick of women. The kind of women who took lush gorgeousness to an art form, while Caroline's beauty was less studied, less polished. Perhaps she was merely pretty, he decided. Not beautiful at all, but pretty.

But then she raised her lashes and speared him with those eyes, and he felt the jolt at gut level. She was an ice queen, and he wanted nothing more than to melt her frigid exterior. It angered him that he did. He'd had no intention whatsoever of touching her, yet here he was, threatening her with the prospect of once more becoming his mistress.

"Why?" she said, her voice laced with the same shock he felt at this turn of events.

Roman shrugged casually, though he felt anything but casual at the moment. "Perhaps I have not had enough of you," he said. "Or perhaps I want to humiliate you as you humiliated me."

She clutched her tiny evening purse in both hands. "You aren't that kind of man, Roman. You can't mean to force me into sleeping with you."

Savageness surged within him. And the bitter taste of memories he'd rather forget. "You have no idea what kind of man I am, *solnyshko*. You never did."

Her lip trembled, and it nearly undid him. But no, he had to remember how cold she was, how ruthless she had been when he'd laid his heart on the line and made a fool of himself over her. He'd trusted her. Believed her.

And she'd betrayed him.

Roman clenched his jaw tight. He'd fallen for her

facade of sweet innocence—but it had been only a facade. He'd made the mistake of thinking that because he was the first man she'd given herself to, she felt more than she did.

I don't love you, Roman. How could I? I am a Sullivan, and you are just a man who works for my father.

He hadn't been good enough for Caroline Sullivan-Wells and her blue-blooded family. Forgetting that singular detail had been a mistake that had cost him dearly. Cost his family. When he'd been forced to leave the States, to return to Russia without a job or any money—because he'd sent most of it home in order to care for his mother— he'd lost much more than a woman he'd fancied himself in love with.

"I have a child, Roman. I don't have time for anyone in my life besides him."

Bitterness flooded him. Yes, she had a child. A son she'd had with Jon Wells, only months after she'd cut him from her life. She'd had no trouble moving on to the next man. Marrying the next man. Roman no longer cared that she had, but when he thought of what he'd been doing in those months after he'd left the States, the resentment nearly overwhelmed him.

His words came out hard. "I don't believe I said anything about a relationship."

Something flashed in her eyes then, something hard and cool—and something that spoke of panic shoved deep beneath the surface. His senses sharpened.

Interesting.

"I won't sleep with you, Roman. Do your worst to me, to Sullivan's, but you won't gain what you think you will."

Neither of them said anything for a long moment. And then, on impulse, he reached out and slid a finger along her cheek. The move clearly surprised her, but she didn't flinch. A bubble of satisfaction welled within him as her pupils dilated and her skin heated beneath his touch. She was not unaffected, no matter that she pretended to be.

"How do you know what I wish to gain, *solnyshko?*" he purred.

Caroline couldn't breathe properly. From the first second he'd touched her, sparks of sensation had been going off inside her like fireworks on the

Fourth of July. Her body ached. Her limbs trembled. And liquid heat flooded her core without the slightest hesitation.

What was wrong with her?

Just because she hadn't actually had sex in forever was no reason to respond to this man. Other men had touched her, yet she'd felt nothing. She'd tried to date a couple of times after Jon's death, because everyone told her she should, and because she was so incredibly lonely without him in her life.

But each time her date leaned in to kiss her, she felt a wave of panic, not lust. The kisses were unremarkable, the touches not worth thinking about. She'd excused herself the first second she could, and she'd never accepted another invitation.

She was beginning to think she was meant to be alone, that she'd only experienced the passion she had because it had given her Ryan. Those days were long over.

Until now. Until the instant Roman had run his finger over her skin, she'd thought she was, for all intents and purposes, frozen inside.

"Why are you doing this?" she asked, her voice little more than a whisper. She didn't want to feel anything for him. Not now. It was too complicated, and she couldn't face the trouble it would cause her.

His ice-blue eyes were intent on hers, his presence overwhelming in the small space of the taxi. His gaze dropped to her lips, took a leisurely trip back up to meet her eyes.

"Why does anyone do anything?"

He was as she remembered, and yet he was different, too. Harder. More ruthless. In spite of what he'd said about not being in love with her, was it her fault that he'd changed? "I'm sorry, Roman," she said, despite her determination not to. "I didn't mean to hurt you."

His laugh stroked softly against her heightened nerves. "Hurt me? *Nyet,* my darling. You did not hurt me. Wounded my pride a bit, perhaps. But I quickly recovered, I assure you."

Caroline swallowed. She'd been devastated after that night, but she'd borne it all with quiet stoicism. Jon had been the only one who'd known what it had cost her to marry him.

She dropped her gaze to where she still clutched her purse in her hands. She'd done what had to be done. She'd been the only one who could. When

Jon's parents had insisted on the match, when they'd threatened to sell their shares in Sullivan's and deliver majority control to a rival who would gut the stores and scatter their employees, Caroline had stepped up and done her duty. She'd saved the family legacy and thousands of jobs. It was something to be proud of. And she *was* proud, damn it.

Too proud to cower before this man.

She lifted her chin and met his hard gaze. She refused to flinch from the naked anger she saw there. And the need. He let that show through for a moment, and it stunned her.

How could he still want her after all that had happened? After the horrible things she'd said in order to make him go away?

But he did. Worse, she realized that she wanted him, too. She wanted to lean in and kiss him, wanted to feel the hot press of his mouth against hers once more. She'd never felt so alive as when he'd kissed her.

But no, that was another time. She'd been younger, more carefree, and unaware of the profound sadness life could bring. She knew better now. If she kissed him—if she let herself fall into him—it would only hurt worse once she had to disengage again.

"I'm glad to hear it, Roman. We weren't right for each other. You know it as well as I."

He snorted. "You mean that you were too good for me. That Caroline Sullivan deserved someone far better than the son of a Russian laborer. The peasant blood that runs through my veins would sully your bloodline."

"I was young," she said, shame twisting inside her at the things she'd had to let him believe that night. But it had been the only way. She'd had to burn the bridge behind her or risk tiptoeing across it again. "And that was not precisely what I said."

"You didn't have to. I understood your meaning quite clearly."

Caroline took a deep breath. There was too much pain here, too many memories. Too many what-ifs. "I know you don't understand, but it was the only choice I had."

It wasn't an explanation, but it was more than she'd said five years ago.

He looked at her in disbelief. "You would dare to say such a thing? To suggest you had no choice in your actions that night? What sort of tale of woe do you intend to ply me with, Caroline?"

Before she could dredge up an answer, the taxi came to a stop and the driver announced over the tinny speaker that they'd arrived at the first destination. Caroline turned her head to stare blindly at the unfamiliar house, before she remembered that she'd purposely given the wrong address.

She drew in a calming breath and turned back to face the angry man beside her. "Good night, Roman."

"I'll walk you to the door," he said, his tone clipped, as she reached for the handle.

"No," she blurted. "I don't want that."

"Then I will wait until you are safely inside before leaving."

Caroline licked suddenly dry lips. "No, don't do that. It's fine. This neighborhood is quite safe. I sometimes take walks later than this just to clear my head."

It wasn't true—the walks, anyway—but she didn't want him to stay, since she couldn't enter the house they'd stopped in front of. She didn't even know who lived here. She knew her immediate neighbors on her street, but not those any farther afield.

Why had she panicked when he'd gotten into the taxi? Why hadn't she simply given her address instead of lying? Now she was caught like a fish on a hook, and he was watching her with more than a little curiosity in his gaze.

"I am not so coarse as to leave a lady on a darkened street. I insist."

He reached across her, intending to pull the handle. She reacted blindly, turning into him and pressing her mouth to his throat. The first touch was shocking. His skin was warm, his pulse a strong throb in his neck, and something soft and needy quivered to life in her core.

She didn't know what she was doing, except that she had to get him away from here before he figured out this wasn't where she lived. She'd wanted to distract him before he could ask questions, but she hadn't bargained on the feelings pulsing to life inside her. She felt as if she'd touched a hot iron. Logic dictated she pull away, but fear drove her onward. An irrational fear, certainly, but she was committed now.

Roman gripped her shoulders and pushed her back against the seat.

"What is this, Caroline? Moments ago, you proclaimed your intention not to sleep with me."

She sucked in a breath. Her body was still sizzling with heat and need from that single contact. What she said next wasn't precisely untrue in light of that fact. "I'm lonely, Roman. It's been a long time, and—and I miss having a man in my bed."

One dark eyebrow arched. "Really? How perfectly convenient."

She reached for him, tried to put her arms around his neck and pull him closer, so she could blot out the maddening voice in her head that screamed she'd lost her mind. She hadn't lost her mind, but she cared more about Ryan than she did herself. She would protect her child with every breath left in her body.

If she'd just given the correct address in the first place, she could've left Roman in the car. But she'd panicked, and if he found out she'd lied, he would wonder why. He would want to know what she was hiding.

Caroline choked on a silent laugh. God, she had

so many things to hide, didn't she? Ryan, her father, the state of Sullivan's finances.

"Take me to your place," she said, her voice raw with emotion. She only hoped he would chalk it up to desire and not fear.

Roman still held her at arm's length, his dark gaze raking over her face as if he could ferret out all her secrets. She lifted her chin and stared back, willing him to believe her. And it wasn't so hard, really, since a part of her *did* want him.

A part she could not indulge, no matter the dangerous game she played.

Roman let her go and told the driver to continue to the address he'd given. Caroline slumped against the seat. She'd thought she would be relieved, but instead the tension in her body wound tighter. She kept expecting Roman to reach for her, to enfold her in his arms and take what she'd been offering.

But he didn't, and that disconcerted her. He should be trying to kiss her, not sitting beside her like a large, silent mountain.

Ten minutes later, the car stopped at another location, and Caroline's pulse spiked. She had to get away from him, had to go home and lock herself

away in her bedroom while she processed everything that seeing him again had made her feel.

"I'm feeling a little unwell," she said, as Roman
swiped a credit card through the reader. "Maybe
I should go home, after all."

Roman didn't even look at her. "If you are unwell, then you must come up and let me get you
something for your…"

"Head," she blurted. "I feel a migraine coming
on."

"Pity," he replied, as he took the receipt the
driver handed to him, and ushered her from the
car before she could think of how to get him to
leave without her.

"You'll just need to call another one," she said as
he led her toward the glass doors of a tall building.
"I really should get home. My child needs me."

"Funny you did not think of this when you were
sitting in front of your doorstep."

"I—I was overwhelmed."

Roman punched in an entry code and the doors
slid open. "By sudden desire for me, yes. I am very
flattered." Except that he didn't sound flattered at
all. He sounded bored. "Now come and take something for your head."

Caroline hesitated a moment, but where would she go if she didn't go inside? This was the financial district at night, not Times Square. The taxis were fewer, the bustle much less. Did she want to stand on the street in an evening dress and frantically wave at taxis?

In the end, she entered the building, walking in silence beside the man she'd once loved, as he led her past a desk staffed with a security guard, and into a private elevator. The ride up was quick, and she was hardly surprised when the doors opened at the penthouse. Roman exited the elevator. She followed, her heart hammering as she stepped inside the masculine space.

A wall of windows lined the entire front of the apartment, looking out over the Manhattan skyline. The space was open from one end to the other, each area flowing into the next: the kitchen with its huge marble-topped island and stainless appliances, the dining room, the living room in which they stood, and onward toward the bedroom she could see through the open door to her right.

Roman left her standing in the living room. She heard the clink of glassware, and then liquid being poured. He returned a moment later with a glass of water and a bottle of aspirin.

"For your headache," he said, when she didn't move to take them from him.

"Oh, yes," she blurted. "Thanks."

She took the water and then Roman shook two aspirin into her hand. She popped them in her mouth and swallowed them down. She truly did have a headache, but it was due to stress and not a migraine.

Roman went and opened a sliding door to a large terrace. After a moment's hesitation, Caroline followed him outside. The night air was cool this high up, the breeze that ruffled her hair refreshing. She'd laid her small purse on a table inside, but she'd kept her wrap. She pulled it tighter and gazed out over the city.

"Is this yours?" she asked.

"*Da.* I bought it over a year ago."

Her insides twisted. "You've come to New York before?"

He'd walked the same streets she had? Gone into the shops? What if she'd rounded a corner one day, with Ryan holding her hand, and bumped into Roman? A chill that had nothing to do with the night air skated over her soul. She felt as if she should have known he was here somehow, but the truth was that she hadn't.

He turned to look at her, his eyes sparkling in the lights from the living room. "Of course. Did you think I would avoid it because you were here?"

She shook her head. "No, but I'm surprised I didn't hear of it before. The press does seem to follow you around."

She didn't purposely seek information about him, but even she could not avoid the checkout stand headlines when they blared something about the sexy Russian and his latest conquest, be it female, business or real estate.

He shrugged. "I am interesting to them because I came from nothing. If I returned to nothing, they would abandon me in a heartbeat."

He could never be nothing, this tall, enigmatic man who made her ache in ways she'd nearly forgotten.

"You've done well for yourself," she said, trying to keep the subject somewhat safe.

Except there was no safety with him.

"Yes," he said, his voice cool. "I know it must be a shock to you and your family. With enough polish, even the filthiest of mongrels can appear well-bred and sophisticated."

His words smarted. She had never thought him beneath her, though she'd let him believe that in the end. Her mother, however, had never approved of her infatuation with him. Both her parents had been nearly frantic with the thought that Caroline would not do her duty and save the stores, when Jon's parents had pushed for marriage.

She'd proved otherwise, but to this day her mother refused to speak of Roman, though she surely knew that her grandson didn't resemble Jon Wells in the least.

"That was a long time ago," Caroline said quietly. "I'd rather not speak of it anymore."

He took a step toward her, closing the distance until she could feel the warmth emanating from his body. Her brain told her to run; her body told her to step into him. She was paralyzed with warring desires—but Roman was not.

He looped an arm around her waist casually, tugged her toward him until she was flush against his body. She shuddered with the burning memories the contact brought up. Flesh against flesh, hard against soft, heat and moisture and pleasure so intense she'd thought she would die.

"Do you wish to forget everything, Caroline? Have you forgotten this?"

His head dipped toward hers, and she closed her eyes, unable to turn away even if she'd wanted to. She didn't want to.

For one brief moment, she wanted to feel this sensation again. She wanted to feel the incredible heat of desire for a man—*this* man—burning her from the inside out. She wanted to feel like a woman one more time.

His mouth claimed hers almost savagely, his tongue sliding between her parted lips to duel with her own. Caroline's knees turned to liquid, until she was leaning into Roman and supporting herself with her hands gripping his strong arms.

He held her against him, his body responding to hers in ways that made her sigh with longing. He demanded everything in that kiss, and she gave it. She didn't know how to do anything else. Roman was the only man she'd ever burned for; shockingly, she still burned for him.

He threaded a hand in her hair and dragged her head back to give him better access. Caroline's hands slid along the opulent fabric of his tuxedo, wound around his neck, her body arching into his with abandon.

She was flung back through time to another moment, another kiss. The first time he'd ever kissed her, they'd been standing on a terrace like this one—only it had not belonged to him. It had been her family apartment on Fifth Avenue, and her parents were having a cocktail party. Roman, as her father's star employee in the accounting and marketing department, had been invited. He hadn't been a member of the upper crust, but he'd stood out in his tuxedo as if he'd been born to be there.

Caroline had never doubted his ability to fit into her world. She'd been flirting with him on and off for the last several weeks. She'd made a point to go through his department every time she'd gone to the Sullivan Group's headquarters.

That night, however, she'd seen a different side to Roman Kazarov. He'd been utterly breathtaking and totally in control. Smooth, suave, compelling. She'd known, watching him talk with one of her mother's society friends, that he was completely out of her league. She was the one who was not sophisticated enough for him.

And so she'd thrown herself at him when she'd found him alone on the terrace. To her surprise, he'd taken what she'd given. And asked for more. Their affair had been hot, passionate, and a little too out of control.

But oh, how exhilarating it had been!

Caroline tilted her hips into his, felt the overwhelming evidence of his arousal. Her knees were already liquid, but now her resolve was following into more flexible territory. Would it truly hurt to spend one more night with him? It had been so long, and she *was* lonely. That had not been a lie.

With a soft curse, Roman broke the kiss. He gripped her shoulders, held her at arm's length. His eyes were hotter than she'd yet seen them. Her stomach clenched, both in confusion and fear. A thread of disappointment wound its way through her as her limbs regained their strength.

"What is this all about, Caroline?" he demanded. "What are you trying to hide?"

CHAPTER THREE

Is the Sullivan Heiress Kazarov's Latest Squeeze?

HIS VOICE WAS harsh, hard, and she flinched from the coldness in it. A moment ago, he'd been kissing her as if nothing had ever gone wrong between them. And now he was back to hating her.

"I have no idea what you mean," she said coolly. In spite of his lethal appeal, she would not fold. She would do nothing except what she wanted to do. And she would win this battle in the end. That's all she cared about: winning.

Thank God he'd kissed her, she thought. Because now she knew she could survive it.

Roman let her go and shoved a hand through his hair. Her lips still tingled from his kiss, and her body still ached with want. It was disconcerting. She realized she was cold and turned to search for the wrap, which must have fallen when she'd gone into his arms. She found it and dragged it over her bare shoulders again, shoring up her resolve as she did so.

"You lied about your address," Roman said.

Her heart seemed to stop in her chest for the longest moment before kicking hard again. Of course he'd known she hadn't given the correct address. "I did. I admit it. But how did you know?"

"Because it is my business to know everything about the people whose companies I intend to acquire." It was said without a trace of irony, as if it was the most ordinary thing in the world for him to know where she lived after all this time. To not only know, but to let her try and deceive him without once saying a word. It made her furious. And anxious.

"You could have said something," she told him tightly. "And saved me the trouble of continuing the lie."

"And miss this charming interlude? I think not. But tell me why you did it."

Caroline licked her lips. Ryan would be in bed by now, his little body tucked under his race car blankets. He would not come bounding out the door. Nor would he have if she'd let the driver take her home in the first place. She'd simply panicked at the thought, and look where it had gotten her. *Fool.*

She needed time to think. God knew she wasn't thinking very well at the moment. She'd been stressed and overworked these last few weeks. There was so much to do, so much to work out, if Sullivan's was to make their next loan payment to the bank. She should be at home, working on the projections before her meeting with the bank tomorrow, not sparring with this ruthless man.

Roman was watching her curiously. And she didn't kid herself that he was anything less than a threat. Under the curiosity lay a tiger waiting to pounce. One sign of weakness, one more mistake in judgment, and she would be toast.

"I lied because I was angry. I didn't want you taking me home." She sniffed. "It was quite a shock seeing you again, I admit. And then you got into the taxi with me, though you were not invited."

He looked dangerous. "That doesn't explain what happened next."

Caroline's face flamed. No, it certainly didn't explain the panic that had made her try to use the promise of sex to distract him. She lifted one shoulder in a careless shrug. Let him think the worst of her. She did not care. "It's not the first time I've thrown myself at you. Perhaps I was feeling nostalgic."

Roman snorted. "Of course. This explains everything."

"And on that note, I think I should go home now," she said, stiffening her spine and facing him with all the haughtiness she possessed. "Clearly, I made a mistake."

His eyes narrowed as he continued to study her. "*Da,* you should go." He strode past her and back inside, where he picked up her purse and handed it to her. Caroline gripped the clutch tightly, embarrassment and fury warring within her for dominance.

Once, he couldn't keep his hands off her. Once, she'd gloried in the knowledge that she could make this man burn for her. Now, he was throwing her out. Which was what she wanted, of course—and yet it pricked her pride, too. No longer was she irresistible to him.

As if to prove the point, Roman's gaze traveled insultingly slowly down her body before finding its way to her face again. "I find that, while you still have the ability to excite me, I'm not precisely moved to take you to my bed."

"What a relief," she snapped, though inside his words smarted. "Though I'm not stupid enough to presume you'll be changing your plans for Sullivan's, I am relieved to know they no longer include me in the bargain."

His laugh was low, deep, sexy, and it sent tiny waves of rebellious delight crashing through her.

"Oh, I still have plans for you, *solnyshko*. Just none for tonight."

Roman stood on the terrace once she'd gone, glass of Scotch in hand, and gazed out at the lights of Manhattan. Though he was on the top floor, he could still hear the sounds of traffic below—the screech of brakes, the sharp clarion of a siren. Somewhere in that traffic, Caroline rode toward her home in Greenwich Village, her perfect blond hair smooth, her lipstick refreshed, her composure intact.

Nothing touched Caroline for long. He'd learned that five years ago. When she'd been in his arms, in his bed, their bodies entwined and straining together, she'd been completely and utterly his.

When they'd dressed again and he'd put her in a cab home—because she'd insisted she could not stay overnight and rouse her parents' curiosity—she'd left him completely behind, forgotten until the next time.

He, however, had lain awake thinking of her. Thinking of how he could make her his permanently. Such a fool he'd been.

Their affair had been brief, a matter of weeks only, but he'd fallen hard. And she had not fallen at all. He'd had a long time to think about why he'd done something so uncharacteristic. And what he'd decided, what he'd realized for the pitiful truth, was that she'd represented something golden and unattainable. He, Roman Kazarov, son of a violent, evil monster and a gentle woman who'd married down, before she'd realized she'd made a terrible mistake, had possessed the ultimate prize in his all-American golden girl.

He'd fallen for Caroline because she'd made him believe his circumstances didn't matter, that his worth had nothing to do with where he'd come from. And then, once he'd believed her, she'd yanked the rug out from under him.

Roman took a sip of the Scotch, let the liquid

scour his throat on the way down. She'd made him forget what was most important in his life. He'd lost sight of his reason for being in America in the first place, and it had cost him dearly. His mother's last months were spent not in the lush nursing home he'd been paying for while he worked at Sullivan's, but in a run-down two-bedroom apartment where he and his brothers did their best to care for her as she slipped further and further into sickness.

He didn't blame Caroline for it; he blamed himself. Acquiring Sullivan's wouldn't bring his mother back from the grave, or change her last months of suffering, but he planned to do it anyway. To remind himself of the folly of allowing anything or anyone to come between him and his goals.

He thought of the kiss he and Caroline had shared tonight, and a tendril of heat slid through his groin. He *had* wanted her. But he'd be the one to decide where and when, not her. And it wouldn't be in his home, the way it had always been before. There'd been something about the way she would come to him, and then leave him replete in his own bed, that had made him feel the difference between their circumstances more acutely.

He'd been the hired help, the poor supplicant in the one-bedroom apartment, while she'd been the heiress breezing in and out of his life. Taking her pleasure and going back to her gilded existence. And to her proper fiancé, as he'd learned too late.

He'd known Jon Wells, though barely. He'd been a quiet man, perhaps even a bit shy. Not the kind to handle fiery Caroline. Roman remembered thinking that she'd been joking at first. Except she'd never laughed, never strayed from what she was saying.

I'm marrying Jon Wells.

But you love me, he'd said, his heart crumpling in ways he'd never thought possible.

It's been fun, Roman, but I don't love you. I never did.

He could still see her face, so wooden and haughty; still hear the words falling from her poisonous lips. Roman drained the Scotch and went back inside. There, he took out the dossier he'd had compiled on the Sullivan Group, and flipped to the section about Caroline.

There was a photo, and a brief information sheet with her statistics and address. There was also a photo of her son, Ryan Wells. Roman forced himself to study the picture, though it always made him feel edgy inside to look at the face of her child with another man.

The boy was blond, like Caroline, and his eyes were blue. Roman looked at the information sheet again. *Four years old.*

It jabbed him in the gut every time.

With a curse, he put the photos away and began to read about the Sullivan Group's latest problems with their loans. They'd taken on too much debt in an effort to staunch the flow of their losses. It wasn't working. Without an influx of cash— major cash—Sullivan's would be pushed to liquidate their assets in order to meet their obligations.

He should let it happen. He should walk away and let the place crumble into oblivion. But he couldn't. He wanted Sullivan's. He wanted every store in their possession—every cashmere sweater, every diamond, every pricey jar of caviar, every last bottle of exclusive champagne. Quite simply, he wanted it all.

But, mostly, he wanted to see the look on their aristocratic faces when he owned everything they'd once thought him not good enough for. He would be the one to destroy Sullivan's. And there would be nothing they could do to stop him.

They only needed a little more time. Just a little, and she could pull this off. Caroline sat in the conference room with her chief financial officer and waited for the financiers from Crawford International Bank to arrive. She'd come in early this morning to work on the projections, and she bit back a yawn as she refilled her coffee.

She hadn't slept well last night. No, she'd tossed and turned, thinking of that kiss with Roman. Thinking of every moment in the car with Roman, and then every moment in his apartment. It hurt to look at him. Physically hurt. He reminded her of everything she stood to lose. And everything she'd gained because of their affair five years ago.

Jon always used to tell her that everything would look better in the morning, once she'd slept on it. At first he'd believed it, and she had, too, when they kept hoping the chemo would make a difference and save his life. Finally, she'd had to admit that the clarity of morning did nothing to erase the doubt and pain of the day before.

Oh, she never told Jon she'd stopped believing,

but she suspected he had, too. Toward the end, he'd said it less and less. Caroline bent her head and swiped at a stray tear. She didn't have time to cry right now. She had to face the bank's financiers and convince them Sullivan's was on the right track to return to profitability and pay their loans. And then she had to deliver on that promise.

Easy peasy.

She waited anxiously while the clock ticked past the appointed hour. The doors didn't open and no one came to announce the arrival of anyone from the bank.

At half past the hour, the phone rang. Caroline snatched it up on the second ring.

"There's a call for you, Ms. Sullivan," her secretary said. "A Mr. Kazarov. Shall I put him through?"

Caroline's fingers flexed on the receiver. *No,* she wanted to shout. *Never!* But she knew, as surely as she knew her own name, that she had to take the call. Roman wasn't calling to discuss last night, nor was he calling to ask about her health. He was calling at precisely this moment for a reason.

A reason she dreaded.

"Rob, can you excuse me?" she said to her CFO.

He nodded and rose to leave. Caroline instructed Maryanne to put the call through as she sat back in her chair and prepared for battle. She didn't know what Roman had done, or tried to do, but she wasn't accepting it lying down.

"*Dobroye Utro,* Caroline." Roman's smooth voice came over the line, and a shiver skated across her skin at the sound of the Russian vowels and consonants. Such a sexy voice, damn him. "I trust you slept well?"

"Perfectly well, thank you," she said coolly, though nothing could be further from the truth. "And you?"

"Like a baby," he said cheerfully, and she wanted to reach through the line and strangle him.

"I assume you're calling for a reason," she said irritably. "Or did you wish to ask me out on a date?"

Roman laughed, and she chided herself for the flood of warmth that dripped down her spine like hot honey. There was a time when his voice over the phone had filled her with illicit urges. She could spend hours on the phone with him then, and had. God knew what they'd found to talk about for so long.

"So impatient. This was always your problem,

solnyshko. Haven't you ever heard that good things come to those who wait?"

"Really, Roman," she scoffed. "Have you taken to speaking in clichés now? Has your English deteriorated? Or perhaps you're just so busy gobbling up companies that you've become too lazy to be more creative."

"I have quite a creative mind, I assure you," he purred into the phone. A lightning bolt of desire shot through her. Her skin grew warm, her body tensing with a sexual ache that made her angry. It was just a voice, for God's sake!

"As fun as this is," Caroline said briskly, "you need to get to the point. I have an important meeting in five minutes."

"Actually, you don't," he said. "If you are waiting for the bankers, that is."

Fear fell over her like a heavy blanket, dousing the electricity stirring in her blood. She didn't need to ask how Roman knew about her meeting. It was clear he did know, so asking would be a waste of breath.

"I suppose you wish to tell me something," she said, cutting straight to it. "Shall I shave my head in preparation for the executioner's ax? Or did you have a slower, more painful death in mind?"

"So dramatic, Caroline," he chided her. "But that is part of your charm."

Caroline ground her teeth in frustration. "And your ruthlessness is yours," she said, so sweetly it made her teeth ache.

"Ah, you speak to me of ruthlessness? Interesting."

Caroline clicked her pen open and closed. Open and closed. "Why is that interesting? You've been traveling the globe for the past two years, collecting companies, and still you aren't satisfied. I'd call that ruthless."

"Perhaps not as ruthless as stomping on a man's heart," he said evenly. There was no hint of emotion in that voice, no warmth or coolness, and she shuddered involuntarily.

"As if you haven't made a second career of breaking women's hearts," she said, her pulse thrumming in her throat, her wrists.

"I learned from the best."

Caroline closed her eyes, willing herself to stay focused. He was trying to rattle her—and he was doing a good job. Since the moment she'd seen him last night at that party, she'd been on edge. Fear, stress, anger, regret—they all coiled together in a giant lead ball in her belly.

"Tell me what you want, Roman," she said. "Why are you calling me now, and how do you know my meeting is canceled?"

"I know because I canceled it."

Her stomach dropped into her toes. "*You* canceled it. And how did you manage that?" she asked, though she feared she had a good idea what he was about to say.

"There is no longer a need to discuss your loans with the bank, *solnyshko*."

"You bought the loans," she said, a lump forming in her throat. She'd known it was a possibility that someone could buy their debt, but her family had been dealing with Crawford International Bank for years. Her father and Leland Crawford had been golf buddies, and she'd had no reason to think he would ever consider selling the loans without first coming to them.

The last time she'd seen Leland, he'd assured her he was in their corner. He hadn't been happy with her father's sudden "retirement," though he did not know the reason behind it. No one did, other than her, her mother and Sullivan's board of directors.

And she intended to keep it that way. Her family didn't need the public scrutiny while their loved one suffered from a cruel disease that robbed him of his memory and his life. The board—some of whom had been sitting when she'd still been a little girl in a school uniform—supported her leadership. Leland knew that much, even if he didn't know the reason. That he would sell the loans without giving her a chance stunned her.

She closed her eyes and breathed deeply. What was done was done.

This was a setback, but it wasn't the end by any stretch.

"You bought the loans, but you haven't bought Sullivan's," she said fiercely. "We are not in default and you can't foreclose."

Roman laughed again, a soft chuckle that made the hairs on her arms prickle in response. "You are not in default *yet*."

Caroline gripped the phone. Hard. "We won't default. I promise you that."

"Very good, Caroline," he said. "Fight me. I like a challenge."

"Really? I would have thought you preferred

your quarry to lie down and roll over before your overwhelming might."

"Oh, I like that too. But only when it's appropriate."

Caroline sucked in a breath. How did he manage to infuse such an innocuous statement with blistering sex appeal?

"I have to go now," she said tightly. "I have work to do."

"*Da*, you have much to do. And when you are finished for the day, you will join me for dinner."

"I think not," Caroline said, hot anger rising in her throat, flushing her skin with heat. "You bought the loans. You did not buy me."

"Think carefully, Caroline," he growled. "It wouldn't take much for your suppliers to cut off your line of credit. If that happens, you will surely default. And then I will own it all. You wouldn't want that, would you?"

"You would go that far?" she said bitterly. "You would interfere with our supply chain in order to win?"

"I think you already know the answer to your questions."

A moment later, the line went dead.

CHAPTER FOUR

Secret Tryst? Sullivan Heiress
Spotted Entering Hotel

BLAKE MILLER THREW her a worried glance as she moved around her dressing room, searching for the right earrings to go with the pink Valentino sheath she'd chosen for the evening.

"Are you planning to tell him?" Blake asked.

Caroline yanked open a drawer and seized the pearl drop earrings she'd been looking for. She was absolutely furious. After her conversation with Roman, she'd had to change into her running gear and hit the company gym for an hour just so she would calm down.

It hadn't worked as well as she would have liked. She was worn-out, but still angry.

She'd had no intention of jumping to Roman's tune, but she'd finally realized that he had her right where he wanted her. She couldn't let him interfere with Sullivan's supply chain, not when she needed every trick at her disposal to make the loan payment on time.

She would go to dinner. But that did not mean she had to like it.

"Tell him what?" Caroline asked as she shoved one of the posts into her ear.

Blake frowned. "About Ryan."

Caroline jerked, her gaze shooting toward the door. But Ryan wasn't there, and she let out a sharp sigh.

"He's watching a cartoon with a sponge character," Blake said.

Caroline tried to smile, though she wanted to chew nails. But not because of Blake. She softened her tone. "You know very well what the name of the cartoon is. We've only had to watch it a gazillion times."

He shrugged. "I know. But I'm refusing to acknowledge I do in hopes I'll be able to forget those horrible songs."

"Good luck with that," she said. "I think they're imprinted in my memory forever."

She finished putting on her earrings and studied herself in the mirror. There were purple smudges

beneath her eyes, and her cheekbones were looking a little sharp. She needed to work less and eat
a little more often, but she'd been so stressed lately
that sleep and eating were not her top priorities.

"Caroline." She turned toward Blake to find him
watching her worriedly. "You didn't answer my
question."

She closed her eyes. "I know." Then she came
over and took his hands in hers. "I love you, Blake.
You're the best thing that ever happened to Jon,
and I love that you're a part of our lives. Without
you, taking care of my little boy these days would
be a lot harder."

Blake shrugged. His green eyes seemed to over-
flow with sadness for a moment, but then he sucked
it in and gave her a smile. "I love you and Ryan,
too. You've kept me sane these last months since
Jon died." Blake squeezed her hands. "He wanted
you to be happy, Caroline. He worried about you."

"I know."

"He regretted that he wasn't stronger when your
parents insisted you marry."

"It wasn't his fault," Caroline said. "He was as
trapped as I was."

She'd always suspected Jon was gay, but she

hadn't really known until he'd told her, after she'd confessed she was pregnant with another man's child. That was the moment they'd become coconspirators and partners in truth.

"But he cost you the man you loved, and he regretted that very much."

They'd talked often of what they should have done, but they'd both known they wouldn't have done anything differently. Jon's parents were ultraconservative, and they would have cut him off without a dime had he confessed his sexual orientation. They'd bought him a wife with their investment in Sullivan's, and once he was married and had a child on the way, they'd assumed everything was well and he was on the proper path.

But you couldn't buy off a cancer diagnosis.

"We both did what we had to do." She pulled in a deep breath. "And to answer your question, Jon is Ryan's father. It would be too confusing for Ryan if he suddenly had a new daddy."

"Ryan was so young when Jon died. He barely remembers him." Blake looked sad. "People often remarry after their spouse dies. Kids get new parents. I'm sure this man would understand the need to protect Ryan until he's old enough to know the truth."

Her heart was a cold lump in her chest at the idea of telling Roman he had a son after all this time. How would she do that? *Hey, Roman, about that last night we spent together before I told you I didn't want you in my life anymore...*

By the time she'd realized she was pregnant, several weeks later, Roman had disappeared from her life as if he'd never even existed. He'd left no forwarding address. She knew because she'd asked Jon to check with Human Resources.

Until two years ago, she'd had no idea what had become of him. By then it was too late to dredge up the past. She and Jon and Ryan were a family, and Roman was a man working his way through women and companies like a rocket blazing across the sky.

"I'm not marrying Roman Kazarov, Blake. Whatever we once had is dead and buried. He despises me now. And I'm not especially fond of him, either."

"He has a right to know about his child, don't you think?"

Caroline turned and grabbed her wrap. Her fingers shook as she put it around her shoulders and smoothed the fabric. "I think it's too late for that. I don't imagine he'd take the news well after all this time. And what if he tried to take Ryan away from me?" She shook her head as a wave of panic swelled inside her. "I can't risk that, Blake."

He sighed heavily. "I know, sweetie. I just wish there was a way."

"I don't think there is," she said with a touch of sadness. "He left before I knew I was pregnant. And then I married Jon. Whatever happened between us is in the past now. And it needs to stay there."

A few minutes later, the car Roman had sent for her arrived. Caroline kissed Ryan good-night, told him to be a good boy for Uncle Blake, and went out to get in the car. The air was warm tonight, but she pulled her wrap tighter and settled into the back seat of the limo. They didn't head south toward the financial district, as she'd expected, but north, toward Central Park. When the car finally stopped, it was in front of an exclusive hotel that faced the park.

Caroline went inside, expecting to find Roman waiting for her in the restaurant, but a uniformed attendant directed her to an elevator instead. She hesitated on the threshold, but then stepped inside. Whatever Roman was up to, it wasn't going to turn out the way he thought.

The elevator disgorged her at the entrance to an opulent suite. Soft music filled the area and a dining table sat near a gently flickering fire. A woman in a crisp uniform came forward and offered to take her wrap as Caroline walked into the room.

"Thank you," she murmured as she handed it over.

Roman sat at a desk nearby, a phone to his ear as he talked to someone in Russian. He didn't sound stressed. No, he laughed—and she almost hated him for it. How smug, how cool, how superior and in control.

He'd always been that way, except that he'd seemed to lose a tiny bit of that control whenever she'd walked into the room. And before long, she remembered, he'd lost the rest of it. Caroline shuddered with the memories that assailed her at that moment: hot skin, cool sheets, and the glorious perfection of his lovemaking.

Things she most definitely did *not* want to think about.

She accepted the glass of champagne someone handed her, and turned away from the man at
the desk. She could see Ryan in him, and it disconcerted her. Last night, she'd been so rattled at
seeing him again that she hadn't paid as much attention to the quirks of movement or the features
that he'd given to his son.

Tonight, in just a few seconds of looking at him,
it was all there. The slope of the nose, the blue
eyes, the stray lock of hair that insisted on falling
forward over his brow, and the way he raked it
back again with an impatient hand. Her heart felt
like a lead weight in her chest. She'd never thought
to see Roman again when he'd left five years ago,
and now he was here.

But what was she supposed to do? Confess everything to him and put her child in jeopardy?
Would Roman try to take Ryan away from her?
Or would he reject his son? Oddly, the thought of
him rejecting her precious little boy was somehow worse than the thought of him wanting to
take Ryan away.

Roman ended the call and stood, all lethal grace
and sexiness in his dark trousers and deep crim-
son shirt. A suit jacket was slung over the back

of a chair, a tie loosened and lying on top of it. He looked so graceful and cool under pressure, and she resented him for it. He had no idea what a maelstrom of emotion he was stirring up in her life. And, she suspected, he wouldn't care if he did.

No, strike that. He would care. He would congratulate himself on it.

"I am happy you could make it," he said in way of greeting.

Caroline stood tall in her platform pumps and cocked a hip as if she were bored. "I don't believe you gave me a choice," she said. "So here I am."

His eyes slid over her. "Yes, here you are."

His gaze felt like a caress, a sensual stroking of her nerves, and she took another sip of champagne to mask her discomfort. "Having your apartment fumigated?" she asked, glancing around the hotel suite with cool disdain.

Roman laughed. "Not at all." He took a glass of champagne from the waiter standing nearby with a tray, and held it high, studying the pale liquid, before taking a sip. "I don't entertain women in my home, sorry to say."

Icy blue eyes speared her with a coldness that made her shiver inside.

"How fascinating," she replied, maintaining her bored tone, though she was anything but. No, her heart thrummed and her skin prickled with heat beneath her dress. She only hoped that little beads of sweat weren't glistening across her brow.

"Yes, and it's all due to you, I might add."

She nearly choked on the champagne. "Me?"

He turned and flicked a hand toward one of the servers. The team melted away, disappearing through a door and leaving them alone in the room.

When Roman turned back to her, his eyes were a curious mixture of heat and coolness—and hatred. Caroline darted her tongue over her lower lip.

"I prefer to keep my affairs away from home these days," he said. "Her bed, her apartment, a hotel. You taught me that."

Caroline swallowed as she thought of all the times they'd made love in his bed, only for her to leave him at the end of it and go back home again. She'd been afraid of what her parents would think if she didn't come home. She'd annoyed him more than once with her refusal to spend the night. She'd hated leaving, but it had been necessary.

"I'm glad I was good for something then," she said evenly. What else could she say?

"You were good for a few things. You could be again."

"I won't be your mistress, Roman," she said firmly, refusing to pretend she didn't know what he was talking about. What he was insinuating.

"Really? Last night, as I recall, you practically begged me to take you to my bed."

Yes, she had. And though it had started out as an act, by the end of the night, when he'd kissed her on the terrace, she'd almost been ready to beg him for real.

"A mistake," she said. "One I won't be repeating."

Roman laughed again, and she found that the sound scraped over her nerve endings and left her trembling.

"This is far more interesting than I'd expected it would be," he said, as he came over and took her arm. Her entire body became attuned to that one spot that he touched, sizzling and aching and wanting more than she'd dared to want in five long years.

How could she be thinking like this when he was a threat to her? When she was absolutely furious with him?

She pulled her arm from his grasp and stepped

out of his reach. He merely smiled and swept out his hand with a flourish, pointing to the table. "After you then."

Caroline went over and yanked out a chair. But Roman was there, ever the gentleman, pushing the chair in for her as she sat. Then he took a seat on the opposite side.

As if they had some kind of radar tuned to Roman, the waitstaff returned at that moment and served dinner, before disappearing again. There was red wine, rack of lamb, delicate new potatoes tossed in cream and butter, and grilled summer squash.

"Eat, Caroline," Roman said, as she hesitated to pick up her fork.

Her stomach was so twisted into knots that she wasn't sure she would be able to eat a bite, but after she tasted the first forkful, she nearly moaned with pleasure as the flavors exploded on her tongue. With the current state of affairs at Sullivan's, she'd been eating on the run for weeks—salads, half sandwiches, the occasional slice of pizza. A real meal, eaten leisurely, was heaven.

Or would be if she had a different dinner companion.

She looked up to find Roman watching her. She dropped the fork as if she'd been caught doing something she shouldn't, and glared at him.

He grinned. "We won't talk business yet," he said. "Enjoy the meal."

"It's fine," she told him, leaning back and crossing her arms over her chest. "Why waste time? The sooner we talk, the sooner I can go."

He lifted his wineglass and took a long sip before setting it down again. "You look as if you've done nothing but business for months. Eating is a pleasure, Caroline. It should be enjoyed, savored. Business will wait."

He cut into his food. She waited for him to say something else, but when he didn't, when he ate as if he was sitting there alone, she picked up the fork and took another bite of lamb. It was absolutely delicious—rosemary, thyme, salt, a hint of garlic, and the fresh flavor of the meat combined into the perfect sensory experience.

Yes, eating was a pleasure. Jon had been a great cook, so good that they'd never hired a chef until he'd gotten ill and needed specialized care. Even now she employed a personal chef, but mostly to feed Ryan something other than takeout. She often ate on the run, while multitasking, and couldn't remember the last time she'd sat down and enjoyed a meal simply for the food alone.

Her free time was spent with Ryan, not savoring meals.

"I don't see how you've managed to create an empire if you stop for leisurely meals three times a day," she said after a long silence. There was sarcasm in her tone, certainly—but also envy.

"Don't forget sex," he told her, his blue eyes suddenly sharp on hers. "I stopped for that, too."

A dull pain rolled through her at the thought of Roman with other women. *Ridiculous.* She knew he'd not been celibate over the last few years. There wasn't a tabloid alive that hadn't detailed his exploits with the various models, actresses, beauty queens and heiresses he dated.

"You are a man of many talents," she said, lifting her wineglass high. "I salute you."

He watched her drink, his gaze following the slide of her throat as she swallowed. A flood of heat rushed through her system, but whether it was due to the alcohol or him she wasn't quite certain.

"Does it make you feel good?" he asked, leaning

back in his chair and studying her like a specimen under a microscope.

Caroline blinked. "What? The wine?"

"No. The rebellion."

She lifted her chin. "I have no idea what you're talking about. Rebellion? Against whom?" She laughed as she shook her head. "You are nothing to me, Roman. Why would I need to rebel against you? In fact, I find the entire notion insulting. I don't need your permission—or your approval—to be exactly who I am."

"How did Jon Wells ever handle you?" he murmured.

Ice crackled through her system then. "Do not speak of Jon," she said, her voice hard. "He has nothing to do with this."

Roman's gaze sharpened as he watched her. "You loved him."

"Of course I loved him! I married him, didn't I?" She didn't know why she said that last. It hadn't been necessary, or even a real reason for her marriage to Jon. Not that Roman knew that. The fire in his eyes banked momentarily before flaring again, fueled by fury and loathing.

Was this really how she wanted to deal with the man who owned her loans? Was it necessary to antagonize him, when he already had so many reasons to despise her?

Caroline folded her arms and willed her temper to subside. "Why are we sitting here pretending to have a civilized conversation, when we both know it's impossible?"

Roman looked so cool it irritated her. "Like it or not, *solnyshko,* I own your loans."

"And what dirty trick did you have to perform to get Leland to sell them to you, I wonder."

Roman's eyes glittered. "You are terribly reckless, aren't you?"

"I don't like to be controlled."

He laughed, the sound soft and somewhat menacing. "Is this how you would behave with Leland Crawford? Or any other bank manager who controlled your debt? Would you accuse them of trickery or be so openly hostile?"

"Leland wouldn't ask about my relationship with my husband," she retorted. "Nor would he imply I needed to sleep with him in order to save Sullivan's."

Roman looked utterly dangerous in that moment. "I've never implied that sleeping with me would save your precious stores. I said I wanted them. And you. That is not quite the same thing, is it?"

CHAPTER FIVE

Where Is Frank Sullivan? While Rome Burns,
He's Nowhere to Be Seen

HER PRETTY EYES went wide, but she lowered her lashes, hiding them from him before Roman could discern her thoughts. Oh, he knew she was angry. And frustrated. Perhaps it wasn't very nice of him, but he enjoyed it.

Since last night, when he'd kissed her, he hadn't been able to stop thinking about before, about all the nights when she'd burned up in his arms. She might be trying so hard to be an ice queen now, but he knew what lay under that cool facade. Heat, fire, incineration.

It angered him to be thinking this way about her, after everything she'd cost him, but perhaps it was poetic justice. This time, he would be the one to take—and the one to walk away unscathed.

The more he thought about it, the more he liked the idea.

"I have a son," she said, her voice firm. "And as much fun as it is to play this game with you, I have to think of him first. I'm not going to be your mistress, Roman. Not for any price."

"Is that so?" He liked her fire, her defiance.

Her cheeks flushed as she stared at him. "If you were a decent man, you wouldn't even think such a thing."

He laughed. "I never said I was decent, Caroline." He leaned forward then, spearing her with a glare. "But I am honest, which is more than you have ever been, *da?*"

She dropped her gaze for the barest of moments, her throat working. And then she was staring at him again, her chin up, her eyes flashing. "I can't change your opinion of me. I'm not going to try."

"That would be a fruitless endeavor," he said coolly. "Especially since you are not being honest now, either."

She looked as if he'd slapped her. Her mouth fell open as she drew back in her chair. She wrapped her fingers around the strand of pearls at her neck and worked them back and forth for several moments before she seemed to realize what she was doing. She dropped her hand to her lap and kept it there, her ice queen demeanor a bit tattered around the edges now.

"I have no idea what you're talking about," she said haughtily.

Her superiority made him want to lash out. "Regardless of what lies you tell yourself, you wanted me last night. Had I not been the one to put a halt to it, you would have begged me to make love to you."

Was that relief he saw in her eyes? Guilt? It was gone far too quickly for him to be sure. "You are much too full of yourself, Roman. I had a moment of weakness, but it wouldn't have gone anywhere."

"Shall we test this theory again?" he growled, a sharp feeling clawing through him. Not for the first time, the feeling she was hiding something prickled to life inside him.

Her eyes flashed. "Is this how you would treat any of the other business colleagues you invite for dinner?" She leaned forward suddenly, her expression fierce. "Would you try to force any other rival to sleep with you, or I am a special case?"

He'd forgotten how passionate she could be when

anger brightened her features. It made the ache in his groin sharper than ever. "I've never said I would force you, Caroline."

She blinked, her righteous indignation stonewalled for the barest moment. "Haven't you?"

He took a sip of wine, enjoyed the rich complexity of the rare vintage as it went down. He loved being able to afford whatever he wanted. He'd grown up with nothing, less than nothing, and he'd watched his parents fight over every little thing. He and his brothers had run wild, stealing food and clothing, fighting with other kids for recreation. Nothing had been easy in his life. Nothing had been handed to him on a silver platter the way it had been to her.

He'd never despised her for it. What he'd despised her for was making him feel, once more, like the son of a violent brute who could barely spell his own name, much less count the coins in his pocket.

When Roman had lost his work visa, he'd lost everything.

And he'd failed his mother, in the same way his father had done when he'd drunk his paycheck every week. There was never enough food, never enough money to pay the bills, yet she'd worked tirelessly to make sure her sons had what they needed. Roman thought of her wasting away in that tiny bed in the grungy apartment he'd had to move her to, and felt like breaking something.

"You have it wrong, Caroline," he told her matter-of-factly, shoving the boiling emotions—the frustration, horror and rage—down deep. "I want you, this is true. But it will be you who comes to me. You who cannot deny the passion still between us."

She made a choking sound. "You are beyond arrogant," she finally managed to say. "And if you expect me to fall into your bed simply because you exist, then you *are* deluded."

He shrugged with a casualness he did not feel. "Nevertheless, it is what will happen."

Because, in spite of her protests, she wanted him. He'd known that from the moment he'd first touched her last night. And even if he hadn't been so attuned to a woman's signals, he could hardly have gotten it wrong when they'd kissed on the terrace.

That had been the kiss of a woman who *needed*.

Her eyes narrowed. "I'm going to enjoy this," she

said, her voice hovering on the edge of ferocity. "Because I will never do what you expect me to do, Roman. You've placed your bet on the wrong pony this time."

He merely took another sip of wine. He did it because it infuriated her. "So you say, *solnyshko.* And yet, we will see…."

She dropped her gaze from his, and he knew she was working on her temper. Working to make sense of everything that had happened between them thus far. When she lifted her head again, he could see the determination there. The fire and grit.

He rather enjoyed the sharper edge to her personality. If she'd rolled over, if she'd cried and begged him to be merciful, he'd have had a harder time goading her.

She picked up her wineglass and took a delicate sip. "I suppose you'll want to discuss the projections," she said, as if the last several minutes of conversation had never happened. "We have exciting things planned at Sullivan's this quarter, and we'll make our next payment on time, I assure you."

"And what does your father think?"

She blinked at him. "My father is retired. He has no opinion about what's going on at Sullivan's."

Roman didn't believe her. Frank Sullivan might have retired and left Caroline in charge of the day-to-day operations of the company, but he was not the sort of man to fade into the background. That wasn't like the Frank Sullivan that Roman remembered. That man had been brilliant. And ruthless once his mind was made up.

"Surely he remains in an advisory capacity," Roman said.

"Your business is with me," Caroline replied firmly. "I am the CEO of the Sullivan Group. My father is enjoying his retirement."

"And what will he say when Sullivan's defaults?"

Her eyes were hard. "We won't default."

Roman shrugged. "I think you will. I've put a lot of money into my research. I don't think it will be contradicted."

"Then why did you take the risk?" she demanded. "Why buy our loans when we won't make the payment? It will cost you a lot of money."

Roman leaned back in his chair. This was the part he loved. The part where he faced an adversary and let them know exactly how vulnerable they were. "I have a lot of money," he said smoothly, shrugging. "I can afford to lose some of it in order to get what I want. Besides, once you default, I will get my money back. Do you wish to know how?"

She looked fierce. Defiant. "Does it matter? You want to tell me, and I'm unlikely to run through the door before you can. Go ahead, say what you so desperately want to say."

He laughed. "I would hardly describe it as desperate. It is merely the truth, and whether you hear it now or later, you will hear it." He picked up his glass and studied the way the wine coated the fine crystal as he swirled it. A good vintage. "I'm going to sell Sullivan's, Caroline. Piece by piece."

Her color flared, but the only betrayal of her mood was the movement of her throat as she swallowed. "And how do you propose to do that? I don't think many companies are in a buying mood for department stores these days."

"Because you've tried to sell, haven't you?" She looked surprised, but he continued before she could speak. "Of course you have. Don't deny it. Just the more unprofitable stores, of course. And no one wanted them. But you were not looking in the right place. Nor were you considering how much the buildings or fixtures would bring if you were to liquidate all of the stores."

She blinked. "Liquidate? Sell the assets?" Her skin seemed to pale in the firelight. "You'll take a loss. In today's real estate market, the property losses alone could be very high."

He shrugged. "Perhaps. And perhaps not. Regardless, I will make money in the end."

Her jaw tightened. "And that's what matters most, right?"

"But of course. What else is there?"

"Tradition," she said softly. "Family."

He snorted. "Sentimentality is not what will get you through this, Caroline. You have to be hard, ruthless, willing to do whatever it takes."

"Like you, right?" Her eyes glittered as she stared at him.

"Don't fool yourself, *solnyshko*. We are all ruthless when survival is at stake. Even you."

"I have a son, Roman. Sullivan's will be his one day. I intend to make that happen."

"Then you will have to be extremely ruthless to make it so, won't you?"

"I suppose I will." She said it like a vow, and Roman's blood thrilled to the challenge in her voice.

He raised his glass. "May the best man win."

"Or woman," she said, lifting her glass and clinking it against his.

Soon after, the waitstaff cleared the table and poured coffee. Caroline didn't look at him as she spooned sugar into her coffee and stirred. He could tell by her color that her temper was still high.

Her hair gleamed golden in the soft light from the fireplace, and the pearls at her ears bobbed delicately as she moved her head. He had a sudden urge to go to her side and pull the pins from her hair. He remembered it cascading over his hands like liquid gold, the light picking out strands that gleamed like fire as it fell through his fingers.

Someone set a plate in front of him, but he didn't look at it. Instead, he watched her. Her chin snapped up and their gazes caught.

"Blueberry cheesecake from Junior's," she said. "Was that on purpose?"

His groin ached. "It was your favorite, as I recall."

"I—" She swallowed, suddenly at a loss for words, and he knew she was remembering the same thing he was. The two of them sitting in bed, eating cheesecake from the box with one fork— and then she'd dipped her finger into the blueberry sauce and smeared it over his nipple.

The cake got ruined after that, along with his sheets, but he hadn't cared.

"You're an evil man, Roman Kazarov," she said, her voice hardening again. "You want me to re-member what it was like between us. You want me to want it again."

Roman smiled coolly. "I never said I fight fair, *solnyshko.*"

No, he did not fight fair. Caroline sat at her desk the next day with the newspaper spread before her and wanted to strangle him.

Love Nest? Sullivan Heiress Spends Cozy Eve-ning with Kazarov

There was a photo of her entering the building, and a speculative piece on what she and Roman had been up to for three hours, followed by a photo of her leaving. My God, they'd watched her go in and then they'd sat there until she'd left again.

And she'd bet every last share she owned in Sul-livan's that Roman had known it would happen.

Why else demand a private dinner? She was no stranger to media attention, but her life had been so sedate lately. Not only that, but she was perhaps also still experiencing a honeymoon period after Jon's death. So long as she was the grieving widow, she wasn't interesting to them.

Drop in a virile, handsome, notorious man, and she was suddenly newsworthy again.

Caroline crumpled the paper and dropped it in the trash. She had a business to run and she wasn't about to let Roman interfere with that. No matter that he was too sexy for words, or that he fed her cheesecake with the sole aim of reminding her of that decadent night they'd once shared. As if she could have ever forgotten. No, she hadn't forgotten, but she'd been determined to pretend she had.

She'd failed spectacularly. Even now, she could see Roman lying against white sheets, his body smeared in blueberry sauce and cheesecake, his manhood rising up proudly while she bent to take him in her mouth and—

Her cell phone rang. She checked the display and then snatched it up, fury—and heat, damn him— pumping into her veins at the sight of his name.

"You think this is amusing, don't you?" she demanded without preamble.

"Hello to you as well," he said, his sexy voice strumming across her taut nerves like silk. "And you cannot allow them to get to you. Ignore it."

"How do you know what I'm talking about?" she demanded, suspicious that he didn't even ask what she meant.

"I have lived closely with the press for the past two years. There will always be stories, Caroline. The trick is not to care."

"Easy for you to say," she said. "And I've lived with them practically my whole life, except they didn't often find the need to humiliate me in their pages."

"Then you have been lucky."

"I get the feeling that's changed," she grumbled. "No thanks to you."

She focused on the computer screen in front of her, a spreadsheet and graphs showing the impossible figure she needed to generate in order to make the next loan payment, in two weeks' time. She'd been so positive she could do it, but now, with Roman in possession of the debt, she wasn't so sure. And that made her feel waspish.

"To what do I owe this unexpected pleasure?" she snapped, turning her chair from the depressing figures and facing the expansive Central Park view instead. It was sunny today, gorgeous, and she wished she was out in it, lying in the grass in the park with Ryan and Blake and a picnic blanket.

"So diplomatic, Caroline," Roman chided, whipping her back to reality with a thud. "When what you really want to do is tell me to go to hell."

"This is a professional relationship. Besides, as much as I'd like to say it, it won't do me any good. You'll still be here, digging into me like a very large and annoying thorn in my side."

He chuckled, and she found herself suppressing the sudden urge to smile. Ridiculous. There was nothing about Roman Kazarov that could make her smile.

"I intend to take a tour of your stores. I want you to accompany me."

He spoke as if it was the most normal thing in the world to say. Her heart tumbled to her toes before beginning to throb. "I can't leave New York, Roman."

He made a noise that sounded like a snort of derision. "You need to. If you narrow your focus to

one store, or to a handful of stores in the metro-
politan area, how will you correct what is wrong
in the others? New York will not carry you, no
matter what you believe."

"I know that," she said stiffly. "But I can't just
take off. I have a child."

"He has a nanny, I presume?"

She thought of Blake, who had been her de facto
nanny since Jon had died. They'd had a girl from
Europe, but she'd left them shortly after Jon's
death. Blake had seemed the natural replacement.
He was an artist by trade, but he hadn't worked on
anything in a very long time.

"Yes, but I won't leave my child for days on end
just to gratify your urge to make me squirm."

There was silence on the other end for a long moment. "Then bring him and the nanny along. You
are a woman of means, Caroline. You can do this."

Yes, she could. But she didn't want to. She could
think of nothing more terrifying than Roman and
Ryan in the same room together. "You don't need
me. I'll send someone with you."

He said something in Russian. His tone suggested it wasn't polite.

And then his voice came over the line again,

hard and cool and oh so commanding in crisply accented English. "This is not a request, Caroline. You will go. I will send a car for you and the boy at five."

"I most certainly will *not*," she said, her heart hot with anger—and fear, she had to admit. Fear for her son. Fear for herself. It was a disaster waiting to happen. "As I've already told you, you bought the loans, not me. I'll send my CFO."

"Send your CFO and watch your supply lines begin to dry up."

"You're a heartless bastard," she replied, turning back to her spreadsheets. Her heart sank just a little bit more at what was written there.

She thought he chuckled softly. "Then we understand one another perfectly, don't we?"

CHAPTER SIX

"I Can't Resist Him," Caro Says as Kazarov
Whisks Her Away for Romantic Weekend

CAROLINE BOARDED THE Kazarov jet at precisely
a quarter to six. She'd sat in her chair after he'd
hung up on her and considered her options. Oh,
she'd been tempted to stay in New York, regardless of what he said.

In the end, she'd decided to be ready when the
car arrived, no matter how furious she was with
the autocratic man who'd sent it. She wanted to
save Sullivan's, so she had to make tough decisions. Do tough things.

Just like always.

Blake and Ryan followed her onto the jet. Roman
was waiting for them in the main cabin. He gave
only the slightest start at the sight of her nanny.
But then he subsided back into the smooth, suave
man she knew him to be. Nothing rattled Roman.

Not for long anyway. And a male nanny was not about to faze him, no matter that it probably wasn't what he'd expected.

Ryan hugged Blake tight, his blue eyes wide as he took in the gleaming interior of the corporate jet. Caroline's heart was in her throat as Roman looked at her child for the first time. *Their* child. She'd hoped Ryan would be asleep when they arrived, and that Blake could carry him into another compartment and keep him there.

But her son had been wide-awake and asking a million questions. The questions had only subsided only when they'd left the car and stepped onto the tarmac. His eyes grew wider as Roman stood, and then Ryan turned his head and buried his face against Blake's shoulder. Caroline put her hand on his back and rubbed.

"It's okay, sweetie. Mr. Kazarov is a friend of Mommy's."

Hardly, but what else could she say?

"You can take him into that cabin back there," Roman said to Blake, his tone clipped. He refused to look at her and Ryan.

Blake's gaze strayed to hers, and she nodded. Once they were gone, she whirled on Roman.

"Do *not* treat Blake as if he's just the hired help. Ryan and I consider him family. Jon did, too."

Roman's eyes were hot. He looked…uncomfortable. It surprised her to see him so tense, but he quickly hid it beneath his polished demeanor.

"I apologize," he said smoothly. "I'm not accustomed to children."

She didn't quite know what to say to that. She hadn't expected such an admission. Or an apology. Which did not make him more reasonable, she reminded herself.

"This was your idea," she told him tightly. "You could have avoided the problem if you'd not insisted I accompany you."

"I am aware of it." He sat down in a plush leather club chair and resumed work on his computer. She stood there, fuming. He'd upended her life in the space of a couple of days—and then made her scramble today as she'd readied her family to travel—and he showed absolutely no remorse for it.

"Have a seat, Caroline," he said, without looking up. "We'll be airborne soon."

She stood her ground. "Where are we going?"

"Los Angeles." He looked up, studied her. "You object?"

"That store is doing well," she said. "I'd have expected you'd want to see one of the underperforming locations first."

"If things are going well in L.A., then perhaps you could determine which lessons might be applied to your other stores."

"You don't want to help me fix things, Roman. So why are we doing this?" She flung herself into a chair and crossed her legs. His gaze strayed over her bare calves, and she found herself leaning toward him, as if she wanted to encourage him.

She leaned back again, deliberately, and folded her arms. What was the matter with her?

His gaze met hers. "This is where you are wrong, *solnyshko*. I bought your debt, and therefore I am concerned about the company's welfare. If you lose money, I lose money."

"Rather defeats the purpose of taking us over, doesn't it? If we default on the loan, it's yours. If we pay up, you have nothing."

"Oh, I don't expect you to pay up. But I do expect to know where the profit is, and how I can turn things to my advantage once you default. I refuse to lose money, Caroline. It's not smart business to lose money."

No, it wasn't smart business. And Sullivan's had been losing money since her father had started to lose his sense of self. She'd done her best to turn things around, but she'd been at the helm for only six months. It took time. Time she didn't have.

She thought of her father and wanted to howl. The loss of his memory had been so subtle at first that they hadn't even recognized it. Forgetting which direction to turn when he left the building. Forgetting where his favorite café was located. Putting his keys in the refrigerator instead of in the bowl by the door.

But then one day he'd left the Fifth Avenue apartment for work—and been found wandering around Central Park hours later, disheveled and confused. He'd recognized her mother, but not her. Not at first, anyway.

"And here I thought you were going to sell it off piece by piece," she said, drawling out the words. "Do make up your mind, Roman."

His smile was as friendly as a hungry lion's. "I still need to know where the money is, darling," he said, his tone as condescending as her mother's after an evening spent hobnobbing at one of her society friends' art auctions.

Really, Caroline, the things that people will buy these days and hang on their walls. Appalling.

Caroline folded her arms and turned to stare out the window as the plane began to roll toward the runway. Within a few minutes, they were airborne, and she opened up her computer to get some work done. She'd just pulled up a spreadsheet when Ryan came bounding into the cabin. Blake was hot on his heels, looking exasperated and a little harried.

"Mommy, Mommy," Ryan cried.

"What is it, baby?" Caroline said, pushing her computer aside and wrapping her arms around her son as he hurled himself headlong into her.

"Sorry," Blake said. "He got away from me."

"It's fine," Caroline replied, hugging Ryan tight. She glanced over at Roman. He'd gone very still as he watched her and Ryan, and her heart climbed to dizzying heights. Would he see what she saw every time she looked at her son? What Blake saw, if the way his gaze kept moving between the boy and the man was any indication?

Caroline breathed in the sweet scent of her child

and squeezed him to her. "What did you want, sweetheart?"

He bounced excitedly. "Are we going to see Grandma and Grandpa in Florida?"

Her stomach squeezed into a tight ball. Jon's parents. Oh, God. They weren't exactly on speaking terms anymore, but Ryan hadn't forgotten them. Jon had confessed on his deathbed that Ryan wasn't his. He'd insisted he had to tell the truth, and she'd understood.

Richard and Elaine hadn't taken the news very well, to say the least. They'd cut off all contact shortly after Jon died. Thankfully, they'd given their interest in Sullivan's to Jon long before then.

"No, sweetie, not this time. We're going to California with Mr. Kazarov."

Ryan turned wide eyes on Roman, as if just realizing he was there. Then he stuck his thumb in his mouth. It was a habit he was getting too old for, but she didn't correct him this time. Everything about this trip was disconcerting to him, so why add another layer of stress?

"Say hello to Mr. Kazarov," Caroline said. "This is his plane we're riding on."

"Hello," Ryan whispered, before turning his head into her shoulder again.

"Hello…Ryan," Roman said, his voice sounding tighter than she'd yet heard it.

Ryan turned to stare at Roman. This time, his blue eyes were intent, his brow wrinkled as he studied the man who'd fathered him. It took everything Caroline had not to fall apart then and there.

"Mommy, he talks funny," Ryan said in a whisper that was not a whisper.

"Mr. Kazarov is from Russia. It's a big country very far away. And I bet he thinks *we* are the ones who talk funny."

Ryan looked puzzled, as if he hadn't quite considered that possibility before. "Can your plane fly to Russia?" he asked.

Roman looked like a man who wanted to be anywhere but here. He was clearly out of his comfort zone, and Caroline started to intervene. But just like that, something shifted in his expression and he was suddenly back in his element again.

"It can," he said. "I have done this many times."

"Can we go to Russia?"

"Someday, perhaps," Roman said. "But not today."

"Maybe we can go see Grandma and Grandpa, too."

"Yes, perhaps."

"Sweetie," Caroline interjected. "Why don't you go with Blake and play with the toys we brought?"

"Will you come play, too?" he asked, his eyes so serious.

Guilt was a hot sting in her heart. She'd been so busy lately, and while Ryan had Blake, Blake was not a substitute for her. "Of course I will. But give me a few minutes to talk to Mr. Kazarov first, okay?"

Ryan nodded and then turned and blazed past Blake, on his way back to the other cabin. Once he and Blake were gone, Caroline looked over at Roman. He was watching her this time, his eyes steady and burning.

"I'm sorry," she said. "He's only four, and more than a little energetic."

Roman shrugged as if it were nothing. "This is to be expected." He paused a moment before speaking again. "He looks like you."

And you, she thought. God help her. But if she'd been worried he would see Ryan and know the truth, she'd just been proved wrong.

"He has his father's eyes," she said softly. Roman's expression hardened, and she felt as if her heart would burst. At that moment, the naked truth punched her with a force she couldn't ignore.

He deserves to know.

He had a *right* to know. And yet how would she tell him? She swallowed. "I'm sorry if he disturbed you just now."

"It's fine." Roman turned back to his computer and tapped a key. Then he was still for a long moment. "I'm not good with kids. I don't know what to say to them, or what they need."

Her throat ached. "They aren't that difficult to understand. Sometimes, it doesn't matter what you say, so long as you simply talk to them. You were a kid once, so think of that."

He swiveled toward her again, and she had to keep herself from recoiling at the look in his eyes. They were flat, dead of emotion. It stunned her, made her want to reach for him and ask him what had happened to put that kind of look on his face.

She did not. Instead, she clasped her hands together and willed herself not to move.

"My childhood was nothing to draw from in terms of how to treat children, believe me. My father was a drunk and a brute. We learned to stay hidden if we wanted to survive."

"Roman," she said, her eyes prickling with sudden tears. "I'm so sorry. No child deserves that."

His gaze was hard, bleak. She wondered what else he might say. Instead, he waved a hand in dismissal, as if he hadn't just said something devastating.

"Go, Caroline. Play with your son. Leave me to work in peace."

A car waited at the airport to take them straight to the Beverly Hills Hotel, where Roman had rented one of the presidential bungalows. It was a sumptuous space, with three bedrooms, a private pool and courtyard, a kitchen, and even an outdoor treadmill and shower. The bungalows were private, sequestered from the hotel in areas where other guests were not allowed. There were gardens, tropical plants and lush greenery that hid the bungalow from prying eyes. It was like having a home in the middle of L.A.

After making sure Blake and Ryan were settled for the evening, Roman insisted they go to Sullivan's now, incognito. It was late, but with the time change from New York, the store was still open for another hour. Caroline dressed in a pair of jeans and a silk tank top before putting on a dark blazer and jeweled gladiator sandals.

She met Roman in the great room, her breath catching at the sight of him in jeans and a dark T-shirt. He looked younger, more carefree, and her heart ached for the man she'd once loved. He used to make her laugh, she remembered. He was serious, but he was funny, too.

She hadn't once seen his funny side since he'd returned. It surprised her how much she longed for it. And how much she still ached over his revelation on the plane. She hadn't been able to stop thinking about him as a small child, cowering from the man who should have loved him instead of frightening him.

They took a rented sports car and drove down Sunset Boulevard. Traffic wasn't thick at this time of the evening, fortunately, though it was still somewhat heavy, and they arrived at the mall where Sullivan's was located in good time. Roman left the car with valet parking and they walked into the store together, a pair of anonymous shoppers on an evening outing.

The store was packed with people even at this hour, and Caroline felt a swell of something approximating pride and relief wash over her. Everything looked crisp and perfect. The salespeople were busy and efficient, and the store oozed the kind of upscale comfort Sullivan's was known for.

Roman went over and stood by the center railing, looking up and down the four levels of the store. People packed the escalators, carrying packages and bags, laughing and talking. It reminded her of everything she loved best about Sullivan's. She hadn't spent much time on the floor lately, because she was always in her office worrying over the figures, but she realized, standing here, that she needed to get into the stores more often.

They were in her blood, and it made her feel more alive than she had in a while to stand here and simply breathe in the atmosphere of happy shoppers and a thriving store.

"Let's go to the food shop," she said suddenly, feeling as if she was twelve again and her mother had told her she could have a treat. "I want something chocolate and scrumptious."

Roman didn't object, following as she led the way down the escalator to the lowest level. The food area was full of shoppers standing at the counters, purchasing the specialty cheeses, the salads, the meat and fish and lobsters, and the various delicacies Sullivan's was known for. The chocolate counter was mobbed, but Caroline was determined. Finally, she managed get to the front and order some truffles. The staff moved efficiently, and though there was a small bit of grumbling here and there, everyone got served in good time.

She and Roman cut through the crowd and made their way back to the escalators. Caroline dug into the signature gold-and-black bag and popped a truffle into her mouth as they stepped onto the escalator to the men's department. "Oh God, that's good," she said, her eyes closing as she chewed.

"Is it blueberry flavored?" he asked, and she snapped her eyes open to find him staring at her.

"No," she said, swallowing. Then she held the bag out. "Do you want to try?"

He reached in and took a piece, sliding it between his lips and chewing oh so slowly. She couldn't seem to tear her gaze from his mouth, from the lips that had once kissed every inch of her body and brought her such unbelievable pleasure.

"I like it better when you feed it to me," he said, his voice silky and hot all at once. "Like the blueberries."

She dropped her gaze away from his, suddenly self-conscious. It seemed as if the noise and commotion around them had disappeared, as if it was suddenly just the two of them alone in the middle of the vast store. "I liked that, too."

Oh God, had she really just said that? It wasn't what she'd meant to say at all. She'd intended to say something along the lines of how the past was the past, no matter how much she'd enjoyed it. But with that one utterance, she'd proved he was right when he'd said she still wanted him.

She did, but she wasn't sure how she felt about it. He was both the instrument of her destruction and the instrument of her greatest happiness.

She should be furious with him. Furious over his arrogance and autocratic ways. Furious over his threats to her business.

But right now, she couldn't seem to summon much fury. No, she remembered him on the plane, his expression stark as he'd told her in a few words that his childhood had been anything but happy.

She wanted to know that man, the one who ached. The one who was still human. The one she'd once loved.

He lifted his hand and pushed her hair away from

her face, tucking it behind her ear. Her entire body focused on that one point of contact, as if lightning had been concentrated in his fingertips. Her blood hummed, her veins swelled and the very air around her seemed charged with electricity.

"Feed me the next piece," he told her, his eyes hot and bright. She hesitated but a moment, her heart thrumming a steady beat that threatened to make her dizzy. Then she dipped her fingers into the bag, withdrew a single piece of chocolate and pressed it between his lips, her fingers sliding into his mouth, over the silky heat of his tongue.

He sucked the chocolate from her fingers, his hot eyes never leaving hers. He'd moved closer to her—or she to him—until she could feel the heat of his body burning into her, though they did not touch anywhere else.

They reached the top of the escalator and she broke apart from him guiltily. Roman, however, took her hand and led her through the men's department to the dressing rooms. There was no one standing nearby, so he dragged her straight into the nearest one and closed the door.

The dressing room was big, but not too big, and the lighting was soft. There were mirrors on three walls, and she backed toward one, holding the bag of chocolate held against her chest. Roman grinned, his eyes bright, and she sucked in a breath as he advanced on her.

"What are you doing?" she squeaked.

"You know what I'm doing, Caroline. And you want me to do it."

Oh, she did. She definitely did.

Her nipples felt tight, and her breath shortened in her chest. Worse, her feminine core throbbed with the ache of sexual arousal. Her body didn't seem to realize there was too much water under the bridge, too much time and hurt between them. And her brain was beginning to think it didn't matter.

Roman backed her against a mirrored wall, one hand on either side of her head, creating a cage from which she knew she could escape if she wanted to.

She didn't want to.

"Do you have any idea how I've longed for this?" he said in a growl, his head so close to hers, his lips firm and sensual as he spoke.

She tilted her head back until it rested on the wall. Her mouth was near his. So near. "Tell me," she said breathlessly.

"You wish to talk?" he asked, moving forward again, his hips crowding into hers, his big body pinning hers to the wall. She could feel his hardness, the perfect leanness of his muscles as he pushed against her.

And then, because she knew there had to be more to it than that, she flexed her hips against his—and felt the hardness she'd wanted to feel all along. He made a sound in his throat that should have frightened her, but didn't. No, it only made the hunger in her body sharper.

She moved her head back and forth against the mirror, answering his question.

"I won't kiss you," he said, his eyes falling to the dip in her tank top, back up again. Hot eyes. Beautiful, ice blue eyes. "I won't touch you at all, Caroline."

"Roman." His name was a plea on her lips. She sounded like a stranger, and yet she was caught in the grip of this feeling. This need for him. It was as if the past didn't exist. As if nothing existed between them except the here and the now.

And right here, right now, she wanted him.

"Kiss me, *angel moy*," he whispered in a gravelly voice. "Touch me. It is the only way."

CHAPTER SEVEN

"They Were All Over Each Other," Man Says—
Kazarov and Caro Spotted Cozying Up in
L.A. Department Store

IT DIDN'T MATTER that she shouldn't do this, that
her sensible side was telling her to stop right this
instant, that it was too complicated and too dangerous. Her wild side wanted to taste Roman
Kazarov again. Her wild side wanted to remember
what it was like to want a man, to need a man, to
lose what was left of her sanity over a man.

But not just any man. Only this one. It had always been only this one.

And so she stood on tiptoe and touched her
tongue to his bottom lip. Just that, so light and
delicate. He tasted like chocolate, sweet and dark
and delicious. And like Roman, heat and power
and sizzling electricity.

"More," he said, and she wrapped her arms

around his neck, sank into him, arched her body into his.

And then she kissed him. It was light, tentative, searching.

Roman would have none of it. His hands shifted from caging her in to holding her face while he took her mouth with all the power and devastation she knew he was capable of.

This was not a kiss. It was a possession. A complete and total annihilation of her resistance. His tongue sought hers, demanded a response—and she gave it. She went wild with it, with the knowledge that she was in his arms once again, that she'd never wanted to be anywhere else.

On some level, she knew her response had only been made possible by what had happened on the plane earlier. By his fear and wariness of Ryan, and by his stark testimony that his childhood had been nothing approximating normal.

She hurt for Roman. It wasn't reason enough to give herself to him, she knew that, but she hardly needed reason when instinct and biology seemed to be enough. She had never, ever been able to resist Roman Kazarov. From the first, she'd wanted him with a violence she'd never felt in her young life.

And once she'd had him, once he'd been hers to possess again and again, the fire had only burned brighter and hotter.

Roman Kazarov was a fever in her blood, a virus she couldn't seem to shake.

His big hands speared into her hair, shaped her head as he held her for his kiss. She made a noise of frustration, of helplessness, as she tried to press herself closer to him. Her body arched into his, and his hands left her head and traveled down her spine, over her buttocks, testing the feel and weight of her as he pulled her into his groin.

He lifted her and she wrapped her legs around his waist, held on tight while he kissed her with all the devastating skill that she knew he possessed. She was wild, wanton, and she didn't care. All she wanted was to merge herself with him, to lose herself in him the way she once had.

He flexed his hips, and she shuddered as lightning streaked through her. Then he pressed her into the wall and, with devastating precision, moved against her most sensitive core until she was wild with need for him.

He was her ruin, her devastation. He was like a hot fire that threatened to burn her as he swept over her. Caroline wrapped her fists into his shirt and tugged it from his waistband.

She didn't want the barrier of clothing between them, didn't want anything but skin and heat and passion.

"Not here," he said, tearing his mouth from hers suddenly. "Not like this."

"I don't care," she gasped.

He set her away from him abruptly, though she nearly sobbed in protest. He held her at arm's length, though she tried to move into his embrace again. Before her body cooled, before she forgot this feeling. Before reality intruded.

His eyes looked almost as wild as she felt. It was a small comfort, but at least he was not unaffected. "You will care, *angel moy*. You will. Maybe not now, but tomorrow you would hate me for this."

She subsided in degrees against the wall, her palms pressed against the cool mirror, and wanted to cry in frustration. Her body throbbed, her nipples were tight little points in her bra, and her core ached with the need to have him inside her, driving them both to completion.

It had been too long. Far too long.

And she would lose her nerve by the time they

got back to the bungalow. Ryan was there, and Blake, and she couldn't see herself letting go, knowing they were in the next room.

She wanted to sob in frustration, but only closed her eyes and breathed deeply, trying to regain her sense of self. It was good this had happened, she told herself. Good she knew her limits.

"I want to go now," she said.

He tipped her chin up, his gaze searching hers. What he saw there must have told him what she was feeling inside. He let her go and stepped back, away from her.

"So this ends here, *da?* You kiss me, want me, but you cannot admit it to yourself beyond this moment."

"It's not a good idea, Roman. For either of us."

"Why should this be? I want you. You want me. How is this a problem?"

She picked up the bag of chocolates she'd dropped, and clutched it to her chest as if it were a shield. "You know why it's a problem," she said, her throat closing over the words. "You hate me and—"

"I don't hate you," he said sharply.

It was her turn to gape. He swore and raked a

hand through his hair, then turned and tucked his shirt in again. The color in his cheeks was high, the sharp blades of his cheekbones standing out in his starkly handsome face.

She wanted to go to him, wanted to pull his head down to hers and just hold him close. Forget, for a few moments, all the pain and heartbreak between them.

She wouldn't, though. She couldn't.

"I left you," she said. "I married another man."

He spun on her, his eyes blazing. "I know this. But in order to hate you, I would have had to love you first. I didn't, Caroline. I only thought I did."

It was a lie.

They zipped through the streets of Beverly Hills in silence, the only sound the roar of the engine as Roman whipped in and out of traffic. He'd told her he hadn't loved her, but it was a lie. He had loved her with everything he had in him. Which, God knew, wasn't much. No wonder she'd left him.

He'd returned to New York convinced he hated her. But when he'd held her in his arms tonight, he hadn't felt hatred. He'd felt lust and want and the urgent need to possess her. Hate had had no place in what he felt then.

Roman made the turn into the hotel and pulled up to the valet stand. Across the street, photographers milled, no doubt searching for the latest celebrity scandal. But he was just as good, so they soon came running over, cameras flashing and microphones at the ready, while he cursed himself for not using a more private entrance.

"Mr. Kazarov, is it true you're sleeping with Bambi Royale? What are you doing in L.A.? Any plans to buy up any stores here? Is Hall's vulnerable?"

Roman ignored them, going to Caroline's side and ushering her into the hotel. She said nothing, but kept her head down and hugged those damn chocolates close as if they were a prized possession.

Why had he stopped her back there? Why hadn't he let her rip his clothes off in the middle of that dressing room, with the public only a thin wall away? It wouldn't be the first time he'd had sex in a risky place.

He'd taken her into the dressing room because he'd needed to kiss her, needed to stoke the fires of her desire for him. He hadn't expected the flame to get out of control, though God knew he should have. If the past was anything to go by, he should have known they would burn hot the moment they touched.

Foolishly, he'd thought he had his desire for her under control. She was just a woman, after all, and he knew how to handle women. But the minute she'd kissed him, he'd gone up in smoke. A small, rational part of his brain had known he couldn't make love to her against the wall of a dressing room—but he'd wanted to.

God, how he'd wanted to.

She'd practically begged him to do it. But he wanted more than a hasty screw in a public place. He wanted to spread her out before him on a bed, like a banquet of delights that he had all the time in the world to sample.

They reached the bungalow and went inside. The house was quiet. She glanced at her watch, as if seeking a way out of an awkward situation.

"Blake has probably put Ryan to bed," she said. "I think I'm headed there, too."

All Roman had to do was kiss her. Step into her space, wrap his arms around her and bend her backward. She would fall, her resolve crumbling like a domino toppling over.

And yet that wasn't enough for him. He wanted more than her surrender. Needed more. But he recognized it would not happen tonight. There was too much between them now, too many raw feelings. She wanted escape; he could see that.

And perhaps it was best for them both. He had to deal with this aching in his chest, this feeling of rawness that had accompanied his outburst that he didn't hate her. He'd lived with the hatred for so long that its sudden absence left him reeling and unsure.

"This is a good idea," he said coolly. "In the morning, we'll go back to the store, only this time we'll announce ourselves."

He had to focus on business, because it was the one thing he understood right now. The only solid foundation beneath his feet.

She dipped her chin to her chest briefly, and then looked up again, her hazel eyes clouded. "That sounds perfect."

"Good night, Caroline," he said, before turning and walking toward his room.

"Good night," she replied, her voice soft and

somewhat uncertain. He almost turned and went back to her. Almost, but not quite. He shut the door behind him and stood there for a long minute. But there was no soft tread on the floor, no knock on his door.

Roman swore softly before peeling his clothes off and climbing into bed alone.

Caroline didn't know what time it was when she finally gave up the pretense of sleep and flipped the covers back. Her heart had been racing for hours now, as if she'd drunk a vat of coffee right before bed. It wasn't caffeine, though. It was Roman.

She couldn't stop replaying every moment of the evening, from the second he'd asked her if the chocolates were blueberry flavored, until the minute he'd turned and walked away from her, only hours ago. She wanted a do-over. She wanted to be cool and aloof in answer to his query, and she most definitely didn't want to slide a piece of chocolate into his luscious mouth.

And she could really do without hot, almost-sex up against a mirror in one of her own department stores. What was the matter with her? Had she lost every last shred of self-respect she possessed? Was she really the kind of woman who abandoned herself in a public place for the sake of a man's touch?

She was very afraid she was, at least when that man was Roman.

Caroline pulled on a robe over her silk pajamas and went to the kitchen for a drink. The house was dark, quiet, the only sounds those of the air purifiers whirring softly in the night and the hum of the refrigerator. She grabbed a cool bottle of sparkling water and twisted off the cap. She stood there for a long while, thinking and sipping the water, until she heard a splash, as if someone was diving into the pool.

She padded over to the glass doors fronting the pool area and slid them open. A man cut through the water in smooth even strokes. *Roman.*

She stood for a long minute, watching the beautiful grace of his body as he swam, the bunch and stretch of muscles, the way his hands barely came out of the water before slicing back in again, propelling him forward like a machine.

He reached the end of the pool, and then disappeared beneath the surface, only to pop up again almost halfway to the other side. He swam for several lengths before he went under and didn't come back up again.

She waited, expecting him to surface, but nothing happened. Caroline's heart did a flip in her chest, and then she stumbled across the pool deck to the edge. Her water bottle—plastic, fortunately—fell to the deck with a crunch as she started to yank her robe off.

He split the surface right in front of her, and she bit back a scream of surprise.

"You scared the hell out of me!" she yelled, her heart hammering, her pulse throbbing hot.

Water rolled down his face. He dragged a hand over his hair, slicking it to his head as he stood in the center of the pool, completely unharmed and unflappable. Caroline wanted to throw something at him. If she'd still been holding the water bottle, she would have used that.

"I did not know you were there," he said smoothly.

"That's not much of an apology," she told him sharply. And then her mouth went dry as she watched fat drops of water slide down his chest and over the hard ridges of his abs, visible above the waterline.

"It wasn't intended to be one."

Caroline closed her eyes for a second. "I thought you were drowning."

"Then I thank you for caring," he said. "I would have thought you might believe it would solve all your problems if I were to disappear."

She started to deliver a sharp retort, but bit it back at the last second. "You're teasing me. That's not nice."

He shrugged and moved toward the edge of the pool where she stood. "Perhaps I am."

Her robe decided at that minute to stop clinging to her shoulders and puddle at her feet. She resisted the urge to snatch it up and cover her body. Not that she was indecent, but the thin silk of her pajamas felt so much more revealing in the middle of the night than her dresses did during the day.

"I was worried," she added unnecessarily. And then she huffed. "Do you have any idea the headache it would cause me were you to drown in my presence? I'm sure there are some who would claim I planned it."

Roman stood beneath her now. He tilted his head back to look up at her. "Then I will be sure not to drown in your presence."

"That is much appreciated," she said.

He grinned. "And now you may want to turn around. Unless you wish to see more of me than you bargained for."

Caroline's throat closed up. *Oh my.* "You're… naked?"

She hadn't noticed that. She'd been standing in the doorway, and he'd been moving too fast. She'd been thinking about the smooth beauty of his body in the water, not wondering if he happened to be wearing trunks. And then when she had come closer, he'd been beneath the surface. She hadn't yet realized…

Oh. My. Heavens.

"There didn't seem much point in putting on a swimsuit at three in the morning," he told her seriously.

It was suddenly too hot. Tiny beads of sweat formed between her breasts, and her nipples beaded tight against her silk top. Roman's gaze narrowed, and she reached up to fold her arms over her breasts. Let him think what he wanted. It was nothing to do with him, and everything to do with the heat and the breeze and—

Damn it, it *was* him. Caroline lifted her chin.

"There are other people in this house," she said primly. "Any one of us might have come out here."

He actually laughed. "Because so many people like to swim at three in the morning. Not to mention the other occupants of this house, besides you, are male."

"Yes, well, one of them is very likely to find what you're displaying quite attractive. Just so you know."

"I'd guessed that already. I'd also guessed that he realizes I am far more attracted to you than to him."

Caroline sniffed. "That's no reason to run around naked, now is it?"

"I like being naked," he said, and her heart skipped a beat. "Surely you remember this?"

"I remember you're an exhibitionist," she said. It wasn't quite true, but she'd never seen anyone more comfortable in his own skin than Roman. "How could I forget?"

His lips curled in a smile. "How indeed? And if you don't wish to see the exhibition, then I suggest you turn around."

She meant to turn around. She planned to turn around. But it suddenly seemed so ridiculous to do so. As if she were a child whose mother had put a hand over her eyes to stop her from seeing something she wanted to see.

She cocked a hip in that bored manner she affected with him when she wanted him to think she was so cool and controlled. "One can look without touching."

"Can one? Interesting."

Before she could answer, or rethink her show of bravado, he rose from the pool in a smooth, liquid move, like a water god rising from the sea.

And she didn't turn away. Water ran down his body in rivulets, over the hard muscles of his torso and abdomen, over his hip bones, down the trail of dark hair that ran from his belly button to his groin, and down the hard, strong legs that propelled him over to the chair where he picked up a towel and rubbed his head.

Caroline's breathing grew shallow. Hot need spiraled inside her belly, flowed into her limbs, melted in her core until she felt rubbery and unable to move. Oh, what a mistake she'd made in not turning around.

A huge, huge mistake.

He still hadn't moved to wrap the towel around

his body. Instead, he dried off slowly, surely, each inch of him more perfect and beautiful than the last.

She was mesmerized. And she realized, standing there with her feet glued to the pool deck, that she hadn't seen a naked man in five long years. Not since the last time she'd seen Roman naked.

He turned and wrapped the towel around his hips, tucking it in until it lay right below his hip bones. And, oh, she wanted to press her mouth there, just there, right beside his hip. And then she wanted to lick her way across his hard abdomen, and down the happy trail to where his thick penis lay.

She would take him in her mouth, feel him grow impossibly hard against her tongue....

"Caroline." His voice was like a whip cracking in her ear.

"What?" she said sharply, her pulse thrumming in her wrists, her throat.

"Don't look at me like that unless you intend to do something about it."

"I have no idea what you mean," she said, bending to scoop up her robe. Except she was far too hot to put it back on, so she balled it up and held it at her side.

He only looked at her, with that superior smirk on his face. Caroline closed her eyes. Damn it, she was tired of pretending she didn't have needs. She wanted to stop being strong, and she wanted to go to him and run her fingers over that hot, smooth skin. She wanted to follow with her mouth, and she wanted to let him do every last thing to her that he wanted to do.

She knew from experience how amazing and formidable he was in bed, and she ached to know that kind of pleasure again.

What would it hurt? What *could* it hurt? They were here, in California, in a gorgeous private bungalow in the middle of the night. If she slept with him once, if she got him out of her system, there would be no need for a repeat.

Then she could concentrate on beating him at his own game.

"You're lying," he said softly when she opened her eyes again, moving toward her on silent, graceful feet. He stopped in front of her, so close but not quite close enough. A drop of water fell from his hair and landed on her silk pajama top, spreading outward over her nipple. Molding what she knew he could already see.

"I might be," she said softly, her gaze on his, her heart pumping hard at the heat in his eyes. "And what if I am?"

"Then do something about it, *solnyshko*. Take what you want."

CHAPTER EIGHT

Caro and Kazarov Setting Up Love Nest?

THE NIGHT WAS oddly silent as they stood facing each other, close enough to touch but neither moving to do so. Caroline's heart was a trapped bird in her chest. She was afraid, desperately afraid, that if she did this, if she moved toward him as she wanted, something would change.

That she would lose a part of herself, irrevocably, if she did. She'd worked hard to forget him—not that forgetting him had been possible. Perhaps, instead, she'd worked hard to put him behind her. Where he needed to be. If she let him back in now, then what?

"Once," she said. "Only this once."

She expected him to agree. She expected him to say *yes, absolutely, now drop the clothing.* What man wouldn't agree if it meant having sex?

But Roman stood there, silent and brooding, and

shook his head slowly, deliberately, until a slow burn started in her belly and rose into her throat, her cheeks.

"Take what you want, Caroline. But understand that from now on, I shall also take what I want. As often as I want. There will be no hiding from what this is, not this time. You aren't going home at the end of the evening and pretending it didn't happen."

His words smarted. And yet she was still thinking about it. Still aching and needing. Wishing there was a way. *Could* she accept his conditions? There was no one to stop her this time, no one to tell her she couldn't have what she wanted.

"You drive a hard bargain," she said, her eyes fixed on his. "Perhaps an impossible bargain."

"Then walk away, my darling," he told her. "Go back to your bed and pleasure yourself, as I am sure you have had to do far too often."

She felt as if he'd slapped her. She thought of lying in her bed, alone, her hands running over her breasts, down her body, her fingers sliding to where she needed them most. It was too lonely, too clinical, to contemplate. Not when he was here, this hot, beautiful, dangerous man who had once known her body so well.

"I—I've not been with anyone in a long time," she told him. It was the truth, but not the whole truth. How could she admit she'd been with no one but him, ever? To admit it would not only make her pitiful in his eyes, it would also give away the truth of Ryan's parentage. And she couldn't do that just yet. Not until she was certain Roman wouldn't do something drastic.

"I understand," he said. "You are afraid. And yet, do I not know you, *solnyshko?* Do I not understand what it takes to make your body sing? Do you think that I could have forgotten this?"

She swallowed the tears that threatened to spill free. "Five years is a long time. And you've had many lovers since."

He put a finger under her chin, tilted her face up until one of those tears escaped and fell from the corner of her eye. "Not one of them was you."

"Don't say things like that, Roman," she chided, needing to bring this back to ground she understood. To less emotional ground. "I might start to think you care."

"I care about making love to you," he said.

"Nothing more. I won't lie to you, Caroline, and tell you this is something it isn't."

"I have no idea what makes you think I'd want more," she said, though her throat ached with emotion. "My, what an inflated opinion you have of yourself."

If she expected him to take offense, he didn't. He just kept watching her with those burning eyes. "Then what will it be? Pleasure? Or a lonely bed?"

She should choose the lonely bed. It was the safest option. And yet she was tired of the safe option. She'd been doing what was best for everyone except herself for a very long time. Though she couldn't say that Roman was best for her, he was at least a choice she could selfishly make. And she wanted him. Terribly.

The only one who would get hurt this time was her.

"Kiss me, Roman," she said, a shiver rolling over her. "Kiss me like you did earlier."

He snaked an arm around her body and tugged her close. And then he dipped his head and took her upturned mouth as if it were a delicacy for him alone. He licked, sucked, teased and tormented— and she knew he hadn't kissed her like this earlier.

Not quite like this, with such heated intention. This was the kiss of a man who was in supreme control, a man who intended to strip her naked and take her body as if it had been made for his pleasure.

"Come," he said roughly, taking her hand and leading her into the house. "I have to wash off this chlorine."

He led her into the master bedroom, and then through the bath and outside to a shower that was surrounded by a tall wall but open to the night sky above. He shed the towel and turned on the taps. And then he dragged her under the water with him, fully clothed.

"Roman," she gasped as the cool water plastered her silk pajamas to her skin. Her nipples beaded tight, and his thumbs flicked over them while he fused his mouth to hers once more.

The water warmed, but she no longer cared that it had been cool. She was anything but cold as flames licked into her. Her hands were free to roam his body, free to caress and cup and feel. It didn't take her long to wrap her hands around him, around that hard, hot part of him she craved.

Roman groaned into her mouth, and she felt a surge of feminine power. For all his strength and hardness, all his ruthlessness, he couldn't remain unmoved here. Not when it was the two of them and nothing but skin and heat and explosive passion.

His hands went to the front of her shirt, and then he was yanking it apart, buttons flying—and she didn't care. He shoved the sodden mass off her shoulders. Her pajama bottoms soon followed, though she had to pull away and peel them off each leg before stepping into his embrace again.

Only she didn't want his hands on her yet. She wanted to make him wild with need, wanted to taste him again. She slipped from his grip like quicksilver and sank to her knees in front of him.

"No," he gasped—but she took him in her mouth before he could stop her. His entire body stiffened as he grabbed the shower wall. Water poured down over them both while she licked her tongue up and down his length. He was hot and hard and satiny—marble sheathed in silk.

"Caroline, *solnyshko*, *nyet*," he said, as she wrapped a hand around him and squeezed.

But she wouldn't stop. The only way to do this, the only way she *could* do this, was to make him lose control first. Because she knew, if he had his way, she'd be writhing and sobbing and begging him for more.

This way, he was the one who begged. He was the one who needed and gasped and lost himself in her. She was relentless, licking and sucking him until he cried out, until his body jerked and he spilled inside her. She took him all, took everything he had to give, and then he shuddered before sinking to his knees and facing her there on the thick tiles.

"That wasn't the way it was supposed to happen," he said, his breath whooshing out of him as if he'd just run a marathon. Caroline went to him and pressed her body fully against his, wrapped her arms around his neck. She loved the sensation of her naked flesh against his naked flesh, of the heat and hardness and slippery feel of the water.

"I didn't realize there were any rules," she told him.

He laughed, the sound rusty and breathless. "If there were, you have just broken them all."

It didn't take Caroline long to realize that she hadn't won a thing by making him lose control first. No, if anything, she'd guaranteed her sensual torture at his hands. He began by soaping her body slowly, thoroughly, his clever fingers slicking over her breasts, her nipples, pinching them softly until she wanted to scream.

Until she was so sensitive she knew she would fly apart the instant he did it again.

Except that he didn't. He left her breasts and moved his big hands down her abdomen, over the faded marks she'd earned carrying her baby. He paused only momentarily there, and it made her heart ache. What was he thinking?

But then he moved on and she couldn't remember what she'd been wondering. He slid one broad hand around to cup her bottom, kneading her buttocks. And then he turned her in his arms until she was facing away from him, until her back pressed into him—and the evidence of his arousal made her gasp.

"Already?"

"I am a man of many talents," he murmured in her ear. "And you have much to answer for."

Caroline shivered in response as he sucked her earlobe into his hot mouth. And then he parted her, his fingers sliding against her, around the sensitive nub she most wanted him to touch. He traced her shape—slowly, deliberately—while his penis pushed insistently against the small of her back.

"Roman," she gasped when his thumb skated over her clitoris. Her entire body clenched in response, aching, wanting, needing.

"All in good time, *angel moy,*" he said. "All in good time."

His mouth was on her throat, her shoulder, his tongue hot and wet against her flesh, his lips firm. His teeth nibbled here and there until she was panting with frustration.

"Are you planning to actually touch me? Or are you too spent and just pretending?"

His laugh was not what she expected. "So demanding, Caroline. I remember this about you. It turns me on."

In response to her frustrated growl, he slid a finger into her body. His thumb skated over her again. And then again, his touch growing firmer each time. Caroline panted and writhed against him, wanting more. It had been too long, far too long, and he was going to kill her before she ever reached the peak.

"Roman, I'm begging you," she finally choked out, when he skated over her clitoris again.

"I like it when you beg."

"Please," she said. "Please. I'll do anything."

He inserted another finger inside her. And then his fingers set up a rhythm, while his thumb moved against her. Her body, already so sensitive, coiled tight, tighter than she'd thought possible—and then she shattered into a million pieces, sobbing his name, her body breaking apart in a way it hadn't in five long years.

He held her while she shook, held her when her body went limp against him, kept her standing when she would have fallen to her knees the way he had done.

She realized he was speaking in Russian, saying things in her ear that sounded so beautiful, but she had no idea what any of it meant.

"Gorgeous," he said, switching to English. His accent was thicker now, and she shuddered with the way the heavy vowels dripped down her spine. So elegant, so mesmerizing.

"I think I should say thank you," she said, when she could speak again. "I needed that very much."

He turned her in his arms and reached for the tap at the same time. The water ceased flowing and they stood there staring at each other in the glow of the wall lamps.

"Don't thank me yet," he told her. "Because this is far from over."

They dried off quickly, and then he swept her up and carried her into the bedroom, despite her protests that she could walk the short distance herself. She pressed her cheek to his shoulder, her face against his neck, and smiled to herself. *Caveman,* she wanted to say.

And yet she loved it. Loved the tenderness and care he showed, as if she were a precious and fragile thing that needed his strength.

When he laid her on the bed and came down on top of her, the fire spinning up in her belly danced out of control again. She reached for him, arched off the bed to press her mouth to his skin, but he pushed her back with a firm hand.

"Not this time," he told her.

He was too quick for her grasping hands, slipping down her body and spreading her thighs apart, his mouth leaving a hot, wet trail along her torso that made her shiver with delight. She knew what he was doing, knew how this would begin, and she didn't think she would survive the sensual torture he intended to mete out.

When he settled between her thighs, she shuddered. He looked up, his eyes meeting hers for a long, intense minute. "You've been wanting this," he said. "Needing it."

She managed to nod.

He dipped to taste her, his tongue sliding along her cleft, making her cry out. She thought she would fly apart. His tongue—his clever, amazing tongue—began to lick into her with the consummate skill of a man who knew how to drive a woman mad. He knew exactly how much pressure to apply, exactly where to press the point of his tongue, and for exactly how long.

He knew when she was close, and he moved his attention away just long enough for the pressure to subside. And then he would return, building the pressure again and again, until she nearly sobbed.

Caroline writhed on the bed, tormented by pleasure, by the need for release—and the certain knowledge that she'd never feel this way with anyone else ever again.

"Roman," she gasped as the spring inside her tightened yet again—

And then she flew free, gasping his name, her back arching off the bed, her hips pressing against that clever, clever tongue.

When she came back to herself, he'd moved until he loomed over her, until she could feel him pressing at her entrance. She drew her legs up high, and then he hooked an arm under one knee and spread her wider, his body now insistently pressing forward.

She tilted her hips, urging him faster, but he swore softly. "I am trying to be gentle," he told her.

"I don't want gentle." She sounded almost petulant, and so very needy.

"I think you need gentle, at least to begin with."

"Roman—"

"Shh, my darling. Just feel. Feel what we do to each other."

Caroline ran her hands down his sides and gripped his buttocks, pulling him toward her as she lifted her hips. His breath hissed in, and she laughed, thrilled to know he wasn't as precisely controlled as he claimed.

"You play with fire," he growled.

"Now," she said in his ear. *"Right now."*

He lifted her toward him and sank the rest of

the way into her body with a groan. Caroline cried out at the sensation of having him fully inside her again. He was big and hard, and yes, her body wasn't quite as prepared for his invasion as she'd thought after five long years.

"Are you okay?" he asked thickly.

"I will be."

He swore and started to withdraw, but she clamped her legs around him and held on tight.

"Don't you dare, Roman."

"For God's sake, stop moving," he ground out.

Rebelliously, Caroline shifted against him again, sensation streaking through her as she pressed his hardness deep within her.

"Caroline, I can't—"

She moved again, more desperately this time— and his control snapped. Suddenly, he was everywhere, slamming into her body again and again, harder and deeper and more intensely with every thrust.

Caroline cried out, but not with pain. The pleasure was too much, too intense, too hot and raw and bold. Roman gripped her hips and held her hard against him, his body riding hers, overwhelming hers—and being commanded by hers, as well.

Their naked bodies pressed into each other, their flesh slapping together with the powerful rhythm they set. Nothing existed outside this bed, nothing but the two of them and the feelings they called up in each other.

Ecstasy was so close, just within reach. Caroline was straining toward it, ready to soar over the edge—when Roman stopped moving. And then a light switched on. It was dim, but she turned her head away from the source, squinting against the sharp intrusion.

"I want to see you," he said roughly. "I want to see your face when you come."

It made her heart beat hard when he said that. It was as if he wanted too much, wanted not only her surrender but also her soul. She had no barriers left at this moment, nothing she could throw up between them to protect herself. She was exposed, raw, her body a creature of pleasure. Addicted to him.

If he sensed her turmoil, he didn't show it. Instead, he dipped his head to hers again, kissing her softly, his tongue sliding into her mouth so sweetly she could have wept.

And then he started moving, more slowly, more

deliberately, stoking the fires within them both until control was again impossible. This time, she could see the pleasure on his face, feel it rising in her belly, tightening everything within her, building to unbearable levels.

She flung her head back as her orgasm slammed into her. It clawed into her belly, her brain, her limbs. It tore her apart and left her writhing on the edge of madness, wanting more of the same, feeling she would never be whole again.

Roman followed her over the edge with a hoarse groan, her name on his lips, Russian words tumbling from him as his release slammed into him. Caroline turned her head against the pillow and sucked in a shaky breath as her entire world seemed to shift beneath her.

Soon, Roman rolled to the side, taking his weight off her. His body was still inside hers, still hard, and she moaned a little at the sensations that rolled through her simply from that connection.

He nuzzled her throat, his lips gliding along her skin, his damp hair against her cheek. She was spent, and yet she could feel new tension beginning to fuse into a ball of panic in her belly. What had she done? What kind of insanity was this, sleeping with the man who'd fathered her child, who was in her life again to take her stores away from her, and who had only ever caused her heartache?

Roman lifted his head to gaze down at her. There was a line between his eyebrows as he frowned.

"What is the matter, Caroline?"

She licked suddenly dry lips. "I should go back to my own bed," she began.

"Nyet." His voice was harsh. Commanding.

"I don't want Blake to know—"

Roman swore and pushed himself away from her. Her body felt cold once the heat of him was gone, and she wanted to call him back to her. But she couldn't.

She sat up and pulled the sheet up to cover her breasts. "I don't know what this is between us, Roman. How can I explain it to Blake if I can't even explain it to myself?"

He raked a hand through his hair. "Why would you need to explain this to your nanny? He is paid to take care of your child, nothing more."

"He's a friend. A-and he was Jon's friend."

Roman's eyes were cold. "This is about your husband? About what his friend will think? My God, Caroline, the man has been dead for over a year.

I don't think anyone can fault you for moving on with your life!"

She brought her knees up to her chest and put her forehead on them. "I don't understand any of this, Roman," she said. "I don't know why I'm here with you. Why I can't seem to resist you, though I know I should. There's too much between us, too much pain and anger, and I feel like this can only end badly for me. For us."

He came to her and pulled her into his arms. She went willingly—too willingly—and wrapped her arms around his torso, burying her head against his chest. She felt him sigh, and she closed her eyes, breathing in the clean scent of his skin.

"Maybe it won't end badly," he said. "Maybe this time will be different."

CHAPTER NINE

Kazarov Leaves a Trail of Broken Hearts in His Wake; Caro Needs to Beware

ROMAN WOKE WITH a start sometime before dawn. He'd barely slept at all, and now he wasn't sure what had awakened him. A dream, maybe. He threw his arm over his head and stared up at the ceiling. Beside him, Caroline slept, her soft breaths whispering in and out regularly. She'd curled in a ball—away from him, he noted.

But she was still here. He remembered what he'd said to her right before they fell asleep. That maybe it wouldn't end badly this time.

He had no idea where that had come from. No, he didn't intend for it to end badly for him—but he did intend for it to end. How it ended for her ought not to concern him.

Except, for a brief moment when he'd been holding her close and feeling her soft body next to his, trusting him, he'd never wanted it to end. He'd wanted to stay just like that, holding her and protecting her always.

Insane.

How could he feel any sort of tenderness toward this woman after what she'd put him through? He'd given her his heart—asked her to marry him—and she'd laughed at him. Pitied him, no doubt. Because he hadn't been worthy of the great Sullivan blood.

For some reason, that hadn't seemed to matter to him when he'd been buried inside her, feeling her excitement, giving her pleasure. Like a trained monkey, he'd wanted only to give her more of the same. More, so that she smiled at him and told him how good he was. So that she kept coming to him for her fix.

Wanting a woman this much was dangerous. He had never made that mistake with any other woman but this one. What was it about him that made him want to throw himself against the same wall again and again in the hopes the result would be different this time? A flaw inherited from his waste of space of a father, no doubt.

That thought made Roman shudder. He was nothing like his father. Nothing at all.

And yet here he was, with the same woman who'd ripped his guts out once before, and nothing was going the way he'd imagined it might. He didn't feel as in control as he'd wanted to feel. He didn't feel as if he was the victor here at all.

He imagined her married to Jon, imagined Jon doing the things to her that he'd done, and it made his inner beast coil and writhe. He could hardly look at their child without wanting to howl. For some reason, the kid hurt most of all.

And Roman had to get over it, because the boy wasn't going away.

He sat up, intending to get out of bed and do some work before it was time to get dressed and go back to Sullivan's. His empire was global, so it was the middle of the workday in some locations. Not that he personally supervised every single company, but he could check in with the managers of those territories and get reports, at least.

And he still needed a plan for the Sullivan Group. He'd bought the loans, and while he intended to honor the terms of their original agreement, he didn't expect they'd make the payment on time.

When he foreclosed, he needed the players in place to do what was necessary to recoup his investment.

"What time is it?" Caroline asked, her voice rough with sleep.

"Nearly six," he said.

She reached out and put a hand on his naked back. Roman felt as if she'd touched him with a brand. "Do we have to get up just yet?"

He turned back to her. "You can sleep, *solnyshko*. There's time yet."

"I wasn't thinking of sleep," she said, and he hardened instantly. It was almost painful how much he wanted this woman.

"What were you thinking?"

Her hand slid over his torso, down his abdomen, and then she hissed when she felt the size of his erection. "That's pretty much what I was thinking," she said.

Soon he was lost inside her, his body driving into hers fiercely, her cries in his ear, her fingers digging into the muscles of his back. He didn't know where she ended, where he began—or how he'd lived the past five years without her.

Something was different now that they'd had sex. Caroline bit back a yawn as they sat in a meeting with the general manager of the L.A. store and his team. She needed to be paying attention to what the man was saying, but all she could think about was Roman. About the way he'd mastered her body last night, and again this morning, giving her the kind of pleasure she'd begun to believe she would never experience again.

He sat across from her at the table, consulting his computer from time to time, asking pointed questions. She should be angry that they were even here, doing this—but she wasn't. He'd been right that she needed to get out in the field and see what was going on. This store was doing fabulously. Part of that was the location, and part was the training and retention program for employees. People here were valued team members, and it showed. Happy employees tended to customer needs, and customers bought in response. They could spend their dollars elsewhere, but they chose Sullivan's based on the level of service they could expect.

Caroline made a note to look into employee practices company-wide. She glanced up again, her gaze sliding over to Roman. He was watching her, his eyes searing into hers, reminding her of all they'd done to each other last night.

All she wanted to do again.

This morning, after he'd taken her to heaven and back at least twice, she'd slipped from his bed and returned to her own room, showering and dressing for the day before Blake and Ryan were up. When she'd joined them for breakfast, Blake seemed none the wiser about her nocturnal activities. Not that she expected he would care, but she still felt a tad awkward about it.

She'd hoped Roman would join them, but he didn't. Instead, he'd passed through the kitchen, said good morning, grabbed a cup of coffee and went to the study. He didn't emerge again until it was time to leave. This time, instead of the sports car, they took a limo to the store.

Now, the manager finished his presentation and the room fell silent. Caroline shook herself, realizing it was up to her to speak. "Thank you, Mr. Garcia," she said. "I appreciate you taking time out for us today. Your store is a model for Sullivan's, and I'll be taking some of your ideas back to the board."

Caroline shook hands with everyone, thanking them for the good job they were doing. And then she and Roman spent a bit more time at the store, touring all the departments before heading back to the bungalow in the limo.

She put her hand over her stomach. It was tight— with worry, with apprehension, with this desperate need she still felt for the man beside her. One night had done nothing to lessen the ache. Not that she'd expected it would, but she certainly hadn't expected to feel even more jittery than before.

"I think that went well," she said as the limo moved through traffic. She had to speak, or burst with the emotions churning through her.

Roman turned. He'd been staring out the window, deep in thought, perhaps, but now he was looking at her with those eyes so like his son's that it made her want to weep. Her heart squeezed tight in her chest. She was going to have to tell him the truth. She knew that now.

Some way, somehow, someday—she had to figure it out. And then she had to be prepared for the fallout. Caroline shuddered deep inside. That was what frightened her most of all.

"It's one store, Caroline."

She toyed with the narrow snakeskin belt she'd put on over her tunic dress. "I know that."

He let out a sigh. "I don't want you to get your hopes up, *angel moy.* Sullivan's is still in trouble."

Her stomach flipped even as she chided herself for it. One night of sex wasn't going to make him merciful, now was it? He still owned the loans, and she still needed the money to pay him so he couldn't foreclose. Besides, she wanted to beat him at his own game, not get special treatment because she'd slept with him.

"I'm aware, Roman. But I'm encouraged." She let out a forceful breath. "We'll make that payment. I guarantee it."

"Let's not talk about business," he said, surprising her with the sudden vehemence of the words.

It melted her reserve. She scooted over on the seat until she was beside him, until she could lean against him and put her cheek to his chest. He put his arms around her, his chin resting on her hair. "We've spent the entire morning and part of the afternoon talking about business," he said, as if offering an explanation.

She ran her fingers along the smooth fabric of his custom suit, breathing in his vanilla-and-spice scent. So handsome. So dynamic. And, for now, hers.

"Maybe not the *entire* morning."

His laugh was soft. "No, not the entire morning. I exaggerate."

He tilted her chin up and kissed her. It was a gentle kiss, the kind of kiss between lovers long familiar with each other. And yet there was that tiny tingle of desire coming to life in her core.

He must have felt it, too, because he suddenly ended the kiss. "We have all night together," he said. "I intend for it to be a long and pleasurable one."

"I look forward to it," she sighed.

He pushed her upright so he could see her face. "Do you? Last night, you seemed uncertain about the prospect of continuing."

Caroline shrugged self-consciously. "I can't say this doesn't confuse me, Roman. But it's time I got on with my life, as you said."

His blue eyes seemed troubled for a moment. "I'm sorry you lost your husband. It cannot have been easy for you."

She lowered her lashes to hide the confusion and guilt he would surely see if she kept looking at him. "It wasn't. Jon was a good man. A good friend."

"I remember him," Roman said, and she looked up again, searching his gaze. "I hardly knew him, but I liked him well enough the few times we met."

"We weren't right for each other," she said, surprising herself that she'd admitted that much. "But we tried."

"For the sake of your child."

She dropped her gaze, nodding. Guilt was a living thing inside her, twisting and churning, making her feel sick to her stomach.

"My parents tried, too. It was a disaster."

She reached for his hand, squeezed it. "I'm sorry."

It was his turn to shrug. "My father was an alcoholic. I doubt that either you or Jon Wells had this problem."

"No." Once more, her heart ached for the little boy Roman had been. He had never shared anything about his childhood when they were together before. She didn't know why he did so now, but she was glad that he did.

He turned his head to look out the window at the traffic. "For him, children were a burden. And a tool to use against my mother. We would have all been better off if she'd just left him. But she didn't."

"Are they still together?"

"In a manner of speaking," he said. And then he turned back to her. "They are both dead."

"Oh, Roman, I'm so sorry."

"This is life. There is nothing to be done about it."

She thought of her parents in their big house in Southampton, of her father slowly forgetting everything and everyone he'd ever known, and wanted to weep. Her mother was handling it bravely, stoically, but it took a toll on her. Her smile, once so genuine and instant, was pasted on now, brittle. As if she needed to cry but couldn't. As if she had to turn a happy face to the world no matter what.

"I've found that life can be very cruel sometimes," Caroline said. "Even when you think you have everything, it finds a way to flatten you."

"Da," he replied. "This is unfortunately true."

He turned his gaze back to the window and they finished the ride in silence. The driver took them through a private entrance so they could avoid the throng of paparazzi that lurked nearby, and for that she was grateful. She didn't think she could take them on, with her heart churning and everything she felt written on her face.

What would they see if they looked at her? A confused woman? A woman who'd never really gotten over the first man she'd ever loved? A guilty woman with a secret she needed to share but hadn't yet figured out how to?

When she and Roman stepped inside the bungalow, she could hear the splash of water, and Ryan's giggles and shouts as he played. Roman stopped in the middle of the great room, hands shoved in his pockets—and her heart pinched tight.

Outside, Ryan was climbing from the pool and Blake was sitting on the edge, watching him. "Want to come outside with me and see what they've been up to?" she asked.

Roman's gaze slid past her. He was frowning. "No. You go ahead. I have work to do."

Caroline sighed. Eventually, she would need to deal with Roman's reluctance to get near Ryan. He wasn't comfortable around kids, but she wanted him to be comfortable with Ryan before she told him the truth.

She went over and slid the door open, and Ryan looked up from where he stood on the pool deck.

"Mommy! Watch what I can do!"

"No running," Blake commanded, as Ryan started for the end of the pool. He stopped running, but his little legs moved fast as he headed to where he wanted to be.

"Watch, Mommy!"

Caroline's heart filled with love as her son screwed up his little face and then jumped into the water with as much concentration as if he'd been performing an Olympic dive. He was wearing arm floaties, so she wasn't especially worried about him trying to swim across the pool. Nevertheless, Blake sat on the edge, ready to spring into motion should Ryan need help.

"Perfect!" Caroline cried as he paddled his way over to where she stood next to Blake. "What a big boy you're turning into. I'm so proud of you!"

Ryan's little face lit up. "I can do it backward, too!" he said. "Uncle Blake taught me."

Blake shrugged when she looked at him. "He did it himself," he told her, sotto voce. "I had nothing to do with it." Then he turned back to Ryan. "Why don't you get out of the pool now, sweetie? Mommy's home and it'll soon be time to eat."

Caroline expected an argument, since Ryan

hated to be stopped when he was enjoying something. But he paddled to the edge even faster. "Can
we have pizza? Please?"

"I think we can manage that," Caroline said.

Blake lifted him out of the pool and grabbed a
towel. "I'll do it," Caroline told him, taking the
towel and wrapping her baby up.

Ryan chattered endlessly while she dried him
off. But then he stopped talking abruptly and she
realized that Roman had come outside. For a moment, she was heartened by the effort. But then
she realized he was standing there with his brows
drawn down, staring at them.

Staring at Ryan. Caroline's heart skipped several beats. "What were you saying, sweetheart?"
she asked Ryan.

He began to talk again, quietly, his gaze darting
to Roman more than once. And Roman had still
not moved.

"There, I think that's finished," she said, wrapping Ryan in the towel again and standing. "Why
don't you go and get dressed so we can have that
pizza?"

"Okay!" He took off running, skidding to a halt

when Blake yelled at him to walk. Blake trailed after him and they went inside together.

Roman was still standing there. Still staring at her. A premonition of fear slid down her spine as she met his gaze. His hot, hard gaze that was filled with something far different than the lust she'd seen there earlier. His face was a thundercloud.

The gathering storm was about to break, and nothing would be the same when it did.

Roman turned and slid the door closed—very slowly, very deliberately—and cut off her only escape. Then they faced each other across the length of the patio. Caroline's pulse thrummed hard. The plants behind Roman began to shimmer. She forced herself to focus on him, forced the blood to keep pumping into her heart, her brain. She would not pass out. She refused to pass out.

"Tell me," Roman said very precisely, "that what I'm thinking cannot be correct."

She tried for cool. "I don't know what you're thinking, Roman."

His eyes blazed as he took a step toward her, his hands clenched into fists at his sides. She sensed that he was on the edge of his control. It was such a far cry from the man he'd been only moments ago in the limousine. She wanted to weep and yell and throw things.

"I have two brothers," he said, his voice diamond hard. "Dmitry and Nikolai. We used to go swimming together when we were children, in the water park in Moscow. It was our summer ritual, our escape." He shook himself, as if he were going deeper into the memory than he intended. "Just now, I would have sworn I was watching one of my brothers. There is something in that child's way of moving, in his expression—"

"He is not *that* child, Roman," she snapped, fury blazing. "His name is Ryan."

"He is your son with Jon Wells." Roman said it as if he expected her to agree, to tell him that the evidence of his eyes was flawed.

The lump in her throat was huge, choking her. There was no way out. No way she could deny the truth now. It wasn't how she'd wanted to do this. Hell, until just recently she hadn't envisioned telling him at all. There were repercussions to telling him, repercussions for more than just the two of them.

"Jon was gay," she said softly, her throat hurting.

Roman looked as if she'd hit him. His face

drained of color, except for two red spots over his cheeks. It took him a long minute to speak. And when he did, his voice was harder and colder than she'd ever heard it. Lethal.

"What, precisely, are you telling me, Caroline? Say it clearly so there can be no misunderstanding."

She sucked in a shaky breath. But she stood her ground, even though what she most wanted was to sink to the pool deck and sob. "You already know."

"Yet I want you to say it." His jaw was hard as he worked to contain the strong emotions gripping him. "Tell me," he ordered, his voice razor-edged.

Caroline flinched. But she didn't shrink from the task. That wasn't her style. No, she delivered the words, knowing she was ripping his carefully ordered world in two as she did so. Knowing this time the rift between them would never be healed.

"I'm saying that I was already pregnant when Jon and I married. Ryan is your son, not Jon's."

CHAPTER TEN

*The Thrill Is Gone? Caro and Kazarov Not
Speaking—Photos from LAX*

ROMAN COULDN'T BREATHE. It took every effort of
will he possessed to make the air move in and out
of his lungs the way it was supposed to do. Every
effort of will not to walk over to the woman who'd
lied to him all these years, and shake her.

Violence rose in waves inside him. Sick, choking, overwhelming urges to wrap his hands around
her neck and squeeze. He shook his head and stood
stiffly, staring at her wide hazel eyes brimming
with tears.

"I didn't know until after you were gone," she
said, as a tear spilled free, sliding down her pale
cheek. "You returned to Russia without leaving
me any way to contact you."

Rage was a living thing inside him. He'd spent
years conquering that rage, years learning not to

be the man his father had been—but right now, he was on the edge of feelings he'd never before felt. He would conquer them, however, because he *was* the better man.

"As if you would have tried," he said sharply. "Do you expect me to believe that?"

She shook her head, and another tear spilled down her cheek. He hardened his heart against the pinprick of agony that caused.

"Of course I don't."

Inside, he was a mess of violent, swirling emotions. Outside, he had to be cool. He had to shut it all down and deal with her like the traitor she was. The traitor she'd always been. He didn't care that she looked miserable—it was because she'd been caught, nothing else.

"I left," he growled, "because I had no choice. Because your father fired me and managed to get my work visa yanked."

She bowed her head for a moment. And then she was looking at him again, her clear hazel eyes spearing into him. "I had no idea. I'm sorry that happened."

Sorry? He clenched his fists at his sides, fighting the urge to howl with rage.

His voice was tight with fury. "I lost everything, Caroline. My job, my home. You. I went back to Russia with nothing. Less than nothing." He swallowed the bile rising in his throat. "It was a...very difficult time."

She spread her hands in supplication. "I didn't want to leave you, Roman. But I *had* to marry Jon." She took a step toward him, her beautiful face etched with pain. "It was the only way to save Sullivan's. His parents owned majority shares at that time, and they were threatening to sell to a competitor if we didn't get married."

Roman stared at her for a long moment, his gut roiling with emotion. And then he laughed. A rusty, bitter laugh. A disbelieving laugh.

"Sullivan's. Of course. It is the only thing that has ever mattered to you."

Her skin flushed. "People were going to lose their jobs. My family was going to lose their heritage. I couldn't allow that to happen."

"Did you sleep with me now, thinking that I would soften and let you keep your precious stores? Because *that* will never happen, Caroline," he finished viciously.

She seemed to deflate just a little. And then her

chin came up. Her eyes blazed. "I did *not* sleep with you for Sullivan's. God knows I'm fully aware that you are too ruthless for that. I've watched you circling closer and closer for the past two years. I've known you were coming for us, Roman. I've always known."

He stiffened. "I buy troubled companies. This is no mystery."

"No, it's not. But you would have come for Sullivan's anyway."

He felt the truth of that statement like the crack of a whip. Yes, he had been angling for Sullivan's for a long time. From the very beginning, he'd wanted to own the company that had nearly ruined his life and made his mother's last days so dreadful. "I'm a businessman. I don't take unnecessary risks."

"But you would have done so to get back at me."

He took a halting step toward her, raw fury breaking through the tight lid he'd snapped onto his composure. She was unbelievable. He was reeling over the fact that he had a child with her, a child she'd kept hidden from him, and she was babbling about her precious stores.

She folded her arms and turned her head away

from him. Her profile was so achingly lovely. The sudden curl of tenderness weaving into his psyche made him angry. He had no room for tenderness for her. No room for anything but disgust.

"You've known where I was for two years at least," he said tightly, "when I took Kazarov Industries global. Why did you not tell me about the child sooner?"

She fixed eyes shimmering with tears on him. "How would I have done that? Jon and Ryan and I were a family then. Not only that, but Jon's leukemia took a turn for the worse soon after you emerged on the scene. I was a bit preoccupied."

Roman didn't want to feel the wisp of sympathy for her rolling through him like smoke. "At least now I know why you lied about your address that night."

She dipped her chin again. "I was going to tell you," she said quietly. "I wasn't sure how or when, but I was going to. Not that you'll believe that, of course."

"I'd say the same thing in your place." He bit out the words. "But it doesn't make it true."

There was a sound behind him. He spun to see Ryan pressing up against the glass, his hands flat on the pane, his eyes on his mother. Roman felt as if someone had punched him in the gut all over again. How had he missed it before? Now that he knew, he could see the kid was a Kazarov. He had the same eyes, the same nose.

But he also had Caroline's features. Roman had noticed that immediately. The narrow chin, the jaw, the blond hair. He'd looked at the boy's picture several times and never seen anything but Caroline. And when he'd seen the kid in person for the first time, he still hadn't seen anything but Caroline and what he assumed to be Jon Wells.

His own flesh and blood, and he hadn't even realized it. What did that say about him?

Ryan looked up at him then, his big blue eyes wide with fear, and Roman's gut clenched. He had a son. And his son was afraid of him. It hurt in ways he hadn't imagined.

He spun back to Caroline. "Why is he so damn scared of everything?"

She moved toward him, smiling, and he realized she was doing it to make Ryan think nothing was wrong. That she wasn't upset. When she stood in front of Roman, blocked from the little eyes at the glass door, she wiped away her tears with the back of her hand. For some reason, her tears hurt.

And that angered him further. Why should he care that she was upset? Why, when she'd stolen his happiness five years ago—and his child, as it turned out?

"He's always been a bit shy," she said. "It's his personality."

Roman closed his eyes and concentrated on breathing in air thick with chlorine and the perfume of plumeria bushes. "Do you have any idea how much this hurts? You telling me about his personality, me needing to ask why he's this way?"

She nodded, and a fresh wave of tears spilled down her cheeks. "I know it does. I'm sorry."

He swore. Violently. The most vulgar words he could think of, the kind of words no good Russian would say without a sense of horror. His mother, if she were alive, would have washed his mouth out with soap. "Sorry doesn't fix a goddamn thing, does it?"

She shook her head. "No."

"There is no excuse for this," he told her, his voice whipping like a lash. He was boiling inside—hurt, anger, fear, all coming together, churning in his gut like acid. "No excuse."

She sniffled, and the sound tore at him. He hated that it did. He despised her. Behind him, the door slid open on its track, and Ryan shot between them, running headlong to his mother and hugging her legs tight.

She put a hand on his still damp hair, stroking it. "It's okay, baby," she said softly. "Everything is okay."

Roman stood there, an outsider, watching the tableau before him. Caroline dropped to her haunches, hugged her little boy to her until he started to squirm. "Are you ready for that pizza?" she asked brightly.

Ryan nodded.

"Then we'll go. Why don't we ask Mr. Kazarov to come with us? Would you like that?"

Ryan only buried his head against her and didn't speak. Roman felt the strength of that rejection as if it were a nuclear detonation inside his head.

"I have work to do," he said, his heart a solid ball of lead in his chest. "Go without me."

She looked uncertain. No, she looked pitying. And that he couldn't take. Roman turned and went inside, blindly finding his way to the study, where he locked the door and then sat in his chair with a thud.

Outside, the world continued the way it always had. But his world had changed. Irrevocably. Now he had to figure out what to do about it.

"We're leaving."

Caroline looked up from where she was going over some reports on the couch, while Ryan and Blake played a game at the table in the dining room. They'd gone out for pizza, but they hadn't stayed away long. The minute the pack of paparazzi swarming around the restaurant figured out who she was, they'd descended, pelting her with questions about her and Roman.

Ryan had started to cry, and Caroline had lost her temper. Roman's driver intervened before she could say anything truly stupid. Then they'd gotten their pizza to go, and hustled into the limo and back to the hotel.

Out of the corner of her eye, she could see Blake look up from the game, but she kept her focus on Roman. She couldn't tell what he was thinking from his expression. He'd managed to hide the raw emotion from earlier behind his usual cool veneer.

She wanted to hold him, but that was out of the question now. "When?"

"In about two hours."

He looked so cold, so closed off, and her heart ached. The truce between them certainly hadn't lasted long. She'd even thought, laughably now, that they might grow closer with time.

He'd never before opened up to her the way he had in the limo this afternoon, and briefly on the plane, when he'd told her about his parents.

Not that she'd ever asked. She'd been young, selfish, concerned with her own drama. She'd been so overwhelmed with love for him, so greedy for his attention, that she'd never asked him any searching questions. She'd thought they would have all the time in the world, back then. She'd only wanted to know how badly he wanted her, how much he worshipped her body. She'd spent every encounter with him thinking of *her* feelings and how to keep him forever.

How terribly naive she'd been.

"Is that necessary?" she said. "It's rather late for Ryan. His bedtime is in another hour."

The coldness in Roman's eyes could have frozen Niagara Falls. "We are traveling on a private plane, not coach class. He can sleep."

She wanted to argue, but she wouldn't. In the scheme of things, disrupting Ryan's schedule by an hour wasn't worth fussing over. And she sensed that arguing with Roman right now was not in her best interests.

"Which location are we going to next?"

She had to have something to focus on, something to prepare for, or she would go insane thinking about all the ways this could have turned out differently.

"We aren't going to any stores," he said.

"I thought that was the point of the exercise." She didn't like the note of panic that crept into her voice.

"That was before." He glanced over at the table, turned back to her with a stony face. "I think things have changed, Caroline. Don't you?"

"I still need to oversee the company," she said. "We have obligations to meet."

His expression grew hard. "You never had a chance, don't you understand that? You can't make the payment, Caroline."

"We still have a little over a week," she said evenly. "And I'm not giving up simply because you say I should."

"You can work from anywhere in the world. You have a computer, a cell phone, video conferencing. I suggest you use them, because we are not going back to New York just yet."

Her heart was a hot flame in her chest. "You can't force me to go with you wherever you like, Roman. This isn't a dictatorship. I have responsibilities. Ryan and Blake have a schedule to maintain—"

He leaned toward her suddenly, his face twisted in rage. "Really, Caroline? You would throw the fact that our son has a schedule I am not aware of in my face?"

Chaotic emotions charged through her, shaking the landscape she'd always stood upon.

Nothing would ever be the same again, she realized. She had a son with Roman Kazarov, and there was no going back to the way things had been only hours ago.

"I'm not throwing it in your face. I'm just pointing out that you cannot uproot a child's life like this."

He looked utterly bleak in that moment, and her heart twisted in sympathy.

"You've uprooted mine," he said, his voice like chips of ice. "We are going in two hours. I suggest you get ready."

CHAPTER ELEVEN

Kazarov and Caro—Will They or Won't They?

CAROLINE DIDN'T KNOW what she'd expected, but the bright blue ocean beneath the plane's wings had not been it. They'd flown through the night and now dawn was breaking and the landscape below was blue. Endlessly blue.

She shook with some terrible emotion, some horrible feeling that he was taking them to Russia and that he would separate her from Ryan. She hadn't considered that possibility when she'd boarded the plane, the idea that he would take her somewhere foreign, where birth certificates and parental rights didn't stack up against the might of a very rich man.

But the ocean below was dotted with green islands, she soon realized. Not the vast reaches of the Pacific then, or at least not the Pacific as it caressed the shores of China and Russia. And soon she comprehended that it wasn't the Pacific at all, but the Caribbean, when she logged on to the on-board Wi-Fi and tracked their flight.

The very real relief that coursed through her was short-lived, however, when she realized that she still didn't know his aim. *Where,* precisely, was he taking them? And what was his purpose in doing so?

When they landed less than an hour later, a van waited to take them to what turned out to be a sprawling private estate. They'd ridden from the tiny airport along empty roads that were lush with tropical foliage, until they came to a complex built on the beach.

"Yours?" she asked Roman as they climbed out of the van. It was the first word she'd dared speak to him since they'd left L.A. so many hours ago.

The house was on one level, but it spanned at least a large city block. A profusion of bougainvillea grew along the front veranda, along with potted geraniums and beds of bird of paradise and flowering hibiscus. Palm trees shaded the yard, and a hammock was tied between two trees where the grass gave way to the white sand of the beach.

"It is," Roman said. She hadn't been certain he

would answer her. It wasn't a warm answer, or even a very friendly one. But at least he'd spoken to her.

"Which island is this, then?" she asked. The airport had been small, with only Roman's jet and a single island hopper that had been boarding when they'd landed.

"Mine."

Caroline blinked. "The whole island?"

His face was dark. "This is an exclusive resort where utter privacy is guaranteed. There will be no more paparazzi harassing you and Ryan." She hadn't realized he'd known about the incident at the pizza parlor, but she should have guessed that he did. "We host movie stars, politicians, heads of state, tycoons. Anyone who can afford the price can stay in one of the villas on the island. This, however, is my house."

She thought she understood now. By bringing them here, he was guaranteeing they wouldn't be hounded by paparazzi seeking a story. They were free to behave as they wished without fear of prying cameras or microphones. No one had to put on a brave face for the press when they were quietly coming apart inside.

"I had no idea," she said, turning to look at the vast stretch of white beach and turquoise water that fronted the house. Palm trees swayed in the breeze, and the tropical sounds of bamboo wind chimes tinkled with each gust.

"I want to go to the beach, Mommy, but Uncle Blake says no."

Ryan tugged at her skirt, his little face screwed up in a pout. Until precisely twenty minutes ago, the child hadn't even known what a beach was.

"Ryan Nicholas Wells," she said firmly, "you know better than to ask me if you can do something when Uncle Blake tells you no, don't you?"

Ryan's expression fell. His lower lip protruded. "Yes, ma'am."

"Now go with your uncle Blake and do as he says."

Ryan kicked his feet in the grass. She expected a tantrum, but a large black woman in a colorful tropical dress came outside just then and invited them in. She carried a tray of brightly colored drinks with umbrellas.

"Banana smoothies," she said. "To welcome you to Isla San Jacinto."

Blake took a drink and handed it to Ryan.

Beach suddenly forgotten, he disappeared inside the house with Blake, sucking his drink nonstop through the straw. Caroline started to follow, but stopped when she glanced at Roman standing so silently, his eyes hard as he looked at her.

Her heart took a nosedive into the floor at the intensity on his face.

"His name should be Kazarov," he said shortly.

"It wasn't an option," she replied, heat throbbing to life inside her. "You were gone, remember?"

If anything, he looked more furious. "I did not precisely have a choice, Caroline. I lost my visa."

She turned to look at the whitecaps breaking near the beach. A tropical breeze ruffled her hair, bringing with it the scent of flowering trees. "But I didn't know that back then."

He snorted. "And yet you were marrying Jon for your precious stores. I somehow doubt you would have told me the truth if it would have jeopardized that arrangement."

She met his gaze evenly. Because she knew he was right. She wouldn't have jeopardized the arrangement, but she would have figured something out. *Something.* "I did what I had to do, Roman."

"And I will do what I have to do," he said.

"You've taken too much from me. I expect to be a part of my child's life from now on. And I expect him to be a Kazarov."

Her heart thumped. "Jon's name is on the birth certificate."

Roman still looked so hard and angry. He took a step toward her, and a trickle of sweat slid between her breasts. It was hot and muggy in the Caribbean, but she wasn't entirely certain that was the cause of the perspiration rising on her body.

"We *are* going to fix this, Caroline. We are going to give Ryan my name the old-fashioned way."

"What's that supposed to mean?" But she knew.

"Don't play dumb with me. It does you no credit."

She tilted her chin up. The breeze ruffled the ends of her hair and, thankfully, cooled the sweat beginning to glisten on her body. "You can't mean to marry me, Roman. You are the notorious playboy, the man who will never settle down. This is not how you want your life to be."

"How would you know what I want? You have never known." He shoved his hands in the pockets of the khaki shorts he wore. His dark hair lifted in the breeze, his icy blue eyes cutting into her. Chilling her.

"We can work this out," she said. "It will take time, but we'll figure it out. You can be a part of his life. I won't deny you that."

Because how could she marry him? How could she be his wife now, after everything that had happened? He loathed her. He would probably always loathe her.

"Right. The way you didn't deny me for the past two years." His nostrils flared, as if he was suppressing strong emotions. "Do you have any idea how much I despise you right now? How much you took away from me?"

She felt his words like a physical blow. "Then why marry me? It can't be good for either one of us."

His smile wasn't meant to be friendly. "You mean it can't be good for you. Poor Caroline Sullivan, forced to marry the Russian peasant, after all. Won't your parents be proud?"

Without thinking, she closed the distance between them and shoved him as hard as she could. He stepped back, surprised—but then he was in front of her again, as solid and as unmovable as a mountain.

She was filled to bursting with the injustice of it all, with everything that she'd sacrificed five years ago when she'd cut him from her life. She'd lied to him then, but she wouldn't lie any longer.

"I loved you, you idiot! I did what I had to do for my family, but I loved you—and I would have defied them to be with you if the price hadn't been so high. If it had just been *me* who would have been affected by the loss of Sullivan's." She was breathing hard now, anger rolling over her in seismic, life-altering waves.

Roman looked stunned. And then his expression hardened by degrees, until she knew he'd convinced himself she wasn't telling the truth.

"Yes, very pretty of you to say. But we know the truth, don't we? Your precious stores will always win, no matter how you try to dress it up in ribbons and bows."

His gaze slid over her, down the open neck of her T-shirt and beyond, to the denim mini she'd donned this morning. She was surprised to see a flare of heat in his eyes—and just as surprised at the answering surge in her feminine core.

After everything.

"You're wrong," she said tightly. "And I *won't* marry you."

His smile made her shiver in spite of the heat. "We shall see."

* * *

He had no idea what he was doing.

Roman watched Caroline and Blake play on the beach with Ryan, and felt like an outsider. He'd told her she would marry him, told her he was doing it to claim his child—and the truth was he had no idea how to be a father. No idea if he even could. He'd had such a lousy example in his own father that he had no idea where to begin.

Bitterness flooded his throat. If he'd been there from the beginning, if he'd watched Caroline grow big with his child, if he'd changed diapers and held the boy at night when he wouldn't sleep, then perhaps he would know what to do now.

He wouldn't be standing here in the shadows of the covered veranda, feeling like an idiot, a stranger to his own child.

Which, he acknowledged, he truly was. The boy seemed terrified of him. Worse, Roman was terrified in return. Not that he would ever admit it. And certainly not to Caroline. She could help him, he knew that, but how could he ask her?

She laughed at something Blake said, and Roman's heart squeezed. He used to love to make her laugh. She had such an intoxicating laugh, the kind that made you want to laugh as well. She must not have laughed much over the last couple of years.

He frowned at the thought of her taking care of her dying husband, a man who had only been only a friend instead of a lover. Had she been lonely? Frightened? Angry?

Roman shook off any feelings of sympathy. She'd lied to him. Kept his child from him. And she would have done so no matter what.

I loved you, you idiot.

He didn't believe it. Not for a minute. She would say whatever it took to make him merciful now. Whatever it took to keep him from destroying her world.

She looked up then, as if she sensed him standing there. He didn't shrink from her gaze. Her eyes met his across the distance. She said something to Blake, and then she was striding across the sand toward the steps leading up to the veranda where he stood.

She walked with an innate grace that had always been, to him, one of the hallmarks of her class. She moved like a woman who'd had every advantage—money, position, power—from an early age. She took it for granted that she belonged, that she was wanted. She didn't think of how people might perceive her. She just *was*.

She was wearing a red bikini with a white shirt tied at her waist, and a straw hat that covered her face. Her skin was one shade this side of golden, yet she wore it better than many of the bronzed women he'd seen on the beaches of his island. She was more beautiful than any of them, including the starlets and models.

Unwelcome heat slid into his groin as she moved toward him, loose-hipped and elegant. It surprised him that he could want her after what she'd done. And yet, when he'd been buried inside her two nights ago, he'd thought there was nowhere else he'd rather be.

"Won't you join us?" she said as she came closer. "We're playing tag."

"Tag." He said it as if the word was foreign, but he knew what it meant. What she was asking.

She nodded. "Ryan enjoys it." She put a hand over the brim of her hat as the trade winds gusted. "It would be a good way to get to know him a little better."

"He's too scared," Roman said coolly. "Of everything."

She shrugged, though he could tell the criticism hurt her. "I told you, it's his personality. He could grow out of it, but you standing here and brooding isn't likely to help. Come play with him. Act like someone fun to know."

He wanted to do it, and yet he couldn't seem to make that first move. What if he failed? What if he proved that he wasn't meant to be a father, after all? If he got down there and the kid shied away from him, what would he do? How would he deal with it?

"I have work to do," he said. "Another time."

She put a hand on her hip. "He'll be in high school before you cease being busy, Roman."

"A multinational conglomerate does not run itself," he said stiffly. Because she was right, and because he was seeking an excuse to avoid making a fool of himself. She knew it as well as he did.

Sadness clouded her pretty eyes. "You have to start sometime. It won't get any easier the longer you delay." She took the steps up to the veranda, coming over to where he stood, and stopping before him. He could see the soft curves of her breasts where the white shirt gapped, the luminescence of her skin, and he wanted to bend and place his mouth just there, where the valley of her breasts started. Then he wanted to lick the curves, slide her bikini top aside and curl his tongue around a tight nipple.

He closed his eyes. No matter how many times he told himself it was wrong to want her, wrong to even consider taking her to his bed again after what she'd done to him, his body refused to get the message. He'd never had a problem quitting a woman—except this one.

Always this one.

She looked up at him then, her blond hair streaming wild and golden over her shoulders. She wasn't the heiress now so much as the bohemian beach girl—albeit a rather pale beach girl.

"Please come, Roman. Ryan is a good kid, but he needs your patience. Within a few days, he'll think you're pretty fabulous. You just have to start somewhere. Why not now?"

He didn't say anything for the space of several heartbeats. And then, because he suddenly couldn't bear the idea of being alone with his thoughts for another minute while she and Ryan and Blake played in the surf, shutting him out, he felt his reluctance evaporate like mist.

"Yes," he said. "I will come."

* * *

The days that followed were as close to perfect as they could be, considering the circumstances. Caroline had decided, that afternoon on the beach when she'd known Roman was watching, that she needed to help him know their child. Roman was uncertain, anguished, and though she might be angry with him for his high-handedness, his arrogance, she owed it to her son at the very least to make sure he had a good relationship with the man who'd fathered him.

She thought of her own father and dark emotion filled her. They hadn't always agreed with each other, but she would give anything to have him back, whole in his mind, and disagreeing with her now. She missed him. How could she deny her son the opportunity to forge that kind of relationship with his father?

She couldn't, and so she'd determined to help Roman navigate the uncertain waters of becoming a parent. For her son, she told herself.

Caroline felt a pang of sharp emotion every time she watched Ryan and Roman together. Ryan had warmed up pretty quickly, but Roman was still uncertain, still walking on eggshells much of the time.

Oh, sometimes he let himself go and just acted naturally—like when he'd taken them all out on his yacht and let Ryan drive the boat, while he'd stood behind the captain's chair, his hands over Ryan's little ones, steering while his son asked a million questions.

Everything about that day had seemed perfect. The sun had reflected like diamonds on the sparkling water, and Caroline had felt as if her heart would burst with delight. Blake had given her an I-told-you-so look, and she'd smiled back at him with genuine happiness, feeling joyful in the moment and wishing it would always be that way.

But, of course, there were too many raw feelings still to be dealt with, too much reality intruding on their lives. Not that anyone had violated their privacy out here. No, that wasn't possible, as Roman had promised.

Reality, however, was always there, in the back of her mind, preying on her thoughts. It was reality that had caused her to pick up the phone and call her mother only minutes before.

"You must return to the city, Caroline," her

mother said firmly. "The newspapers are simply filled with gossip about you and that horrid man. I've had to hide them from your father. It would kill him to think that Roman Kazarov might soon be running his stores."

Caroline closed her eyes and pressed two fingers to her temples. As if her father would even remember who Roman was. "Mother, the reality is that Daddy made some poor decisions and we're in pretty deep. I'm trying to fix it, but it's not easy."

They had only days left, and she had all her people working overtime. Even she was putting in overtime, spending long hours with her spreadsheets and her telephone when she wasn't helping Roman get to know his son. The numbers were still dismal—and she was tired and numb and ready to give up.

Except that every time she thought that, she got angry with herself. She was *not* giving up. Her father wouldn't if he were here. Jon wouldn't have, either. A few more days. They'd need a miracle, but anything was possible. She'd been calling everyone she could think of, searching for investors. She'd found few.

Her mother sniffed in that aristocratic way she

had. Jessica Hartshorne Sullivan came from a very old and venerable New York family, and though some in her set had considered her to have married down when she'd chosen a businessman like Frank Sullivan, she'd never once given the slightest indication she agreed with them.

Considering her reaction to Roman, it was, in many ways, pure irony. Not that Caroline planned to point it out to her.

"Some days, he wants to go into the office."

Caroline could hear the wistfulness in her mother's voice, and sadness clawed at her. Her father, once so vibrant, was a shell of himself now. It wasn't fair.

"That's not possible, Mother, and you know it."

She heard her mother sniff again, only this time it was due to a far more identifiable emotion. "It's been…difficult," she said, her voice becoming thready. "Even with the nurse. It's happening far more quickly than I would have believed, Caroline. Just yesterday, he looked at me like I was a stranger. He forgets my name more often now…."

Caroline put her head in her free hand as her eyes filled with tears. "I'm sorry, Mother. All we can do is make sure he's taken care of, that he's safe and happy."

They spoke for a few more minutes, and then Caroline ended the call. She felt so bleak inside, so ravaged. There was nothing she could do to fix this. She felt she should be there at her mother's side, and yet it wouldn't change a thing if she were. When she'd suggested she should come to Southampton, her mother had waved the thought away as if it was nonsense. She wanted Caroline in New York, away from Roman Kazarov and the tabloids, not in Southampton.

Caroline grabbed a tissue and wiped her eyes. When she looked up, Roman was there. A dark frown rode his handsome face. His gaze grew sharper as their eyes met. She wondered how long he'd been standing in the entry.

"What is wrong, Caroline? Has something happened to your father?"

She started to shake her head, denial coming automatically—but she couldn't seem to complete the movement. Instead, to her horror, she burst into tears.

CHAPTER TWELVE

Has the Billionaire Playboy Been Tamed at Last?

THAT HE came to her side and pulled her into his arms should have comforted her. And it did, except that it also made her sob all the harder. It wasn't just for her father she cried. It was for Roman, for her and their child, for Jon and Blake. For everything that had been lost over the years—and everything yet to be lost.

"I—I'm sorry," she said, her face against his chest, her fingers clutching his dark shirt. He was so warm and solid, so *there* when the rest of the world seemed to be doing its damnedest to work against her at that precise moment.

His fingers traced a slow, sensual path up her spine. Not that he meant the touch to be anything other than comforting, she was certain, but her body reacted anyway. Her nipples tightened, and

her feminine core flooded with heat and moisture and the kind of need that only he could call
up within her.

Blindly, she tilted her head back and went up on
her tiptoes to kiss him. He stiffened—and then
he groaned and she was in his arms, really in his
arms, and he was kissing her as if he'd been dying
without her.

His big hands shaped her waist, traveled along
her ribs and up to cup the swells of her breasts.
When his thumbs flicked across her nipples, she
moaned and arched herself into his hands.

So quickly she became his to command, his to do
with as he wanted. It had been over a week since
they'd made love in L.A., and she was dying for
him as if it had been a century. She'd thought he
would never want to touch her again. But he did,
he was, and she was filled with a fierce joy that
he still desired her.

She had to have him inside her again. Now. Her
fingers went to the waistband of his board shorts.
He made a sound in his throat—and then he set
her away from him.

"Stop," he told her hoarsely.

She staggered backward until her butt was

against the edge of the desk she'd been sitting at only moments before. She could only gape up at him with wide, wounded eyes.

"Chert poberi," he said, dragging a hand through his hair. "I want you, God help me, but not like this. Not when you are crying and upset."

Caroline pulled in a shaky breath as her brain focused on those three little words. He wanted her. He *still* wanted her. She dropped her gaze. Inside, she was a churning, roiling mess of conflicting emotions. Something was breaking inside her, something monumental. Something she was afraid to examine.

And it had to do with this man. With the knowledge that it wasn't quite as ruined between them as she'd thought.

He put his hands on her shoulders, squeezed, and she nearly broke down once more.

"Can you tell me what is wrong?" His voice was almost tender.

She hesitated. If she let the words out, then what? But he knew something was wrong, and if she didn't say anything, he'd only grow suspicious. "M-my father is sick." That much was true.

Roman tipped her chin up with a finger. "Then you must go to his side."

Her eyes filled again. The concern she saw in his gaze would be her undoing. She was still scrambling to protect her family, and he wanted to help her in spite of everything the Sullivans had done to him.

"It's not necessary." She bit her lip. How could she explain without giving it all away? "It's chronic, and while he won't get better, it won't kill him either. He most likely has many years left. It's just…hard."

"This is why he retired?"

She nodded. "He had to. There is no way he could continue working."

Roman looked troubled. "I'm sorry, Caroline."

She was tired of beating her head against the wall, tired of fighting and working and getting nowhere fast. "You're right that he made bad decisions at Sullivan's, but we didn't know he was ill. I've been trying to put it back together. But soon it won't matter, right?" She smiled, though her mouth trembled at the corners. "You will do what you usually do, and Sullivan's will be finished."

He looked fierce for a moment. And then he

dragged her into his arms again. She slipped her arms around his waist and just stood with her head against him, breathing in his scent. He smelled like salt water and sun, alive and vibrant and delicious.

He was solid, and here, and she was suddenly glad of it.

"It's not like you to give up so easily," he said after a while. "What happened to that fierce determination to beat me at my own game?"

She sighed. It wasn't that she didn't want to save her family legacy. She just wanted it to be simpler, to not hurt so much or exact such a price. Who was she doing it for, anyway? She'd always thought it was for her family, for herself. And now for Ryan. But if it went away, what had she really lost? Compared to a father, a husband, the man she'd once lived for as if he were the entire world?

So long as she had Ryan, she had everything she needed. Maybe it was time to break from the chains of the past and let life roll along unfettered for a while.

"I'm tired, Roman," she said. "Sullivan's has cost me too much over the years. Maybe it's time for someone else to take the responsibility. Rather than breaking it up, maybe you could absorb it into your company and keep some of the better stores open."

He was silent for so long she began to wonder if he'd heard her. But then he spoke. "You're only saying this because you are upset. Another hour, and you'll be fighting again. Sullivan's is in your blood."

"I wish it wasn't," she said fiercely, because on some level she knew he was right.

But she meant it. For once, she truly wanted free of the burden. She'd done so much, fought so hard—and the mountain only seemed to grow taller. She felt like Sisyphus, condemned to roll the same damn rock up the same damn mountain, only to watch it roll back down again once she'd reached the pinnacle.

There had to be something better in life, right? Something more important? She could feel Roman's heart beating beneath her ear, the rhythmic pulse strong and steady, and she knew with a certainly what that something was.

Love. Family. Joy.

She knew then what this fierce restlessness was: she still loved him. It was a jubilant realization—and a sobering one. She loved this man, had always loved him—and yet she'd betrayed him. Betrayed them both.

She'd taken what he'd felt for her and shattered it like a piece of fine crystal dropped from a great height.

Fear curled around her heart then. How could you ever reassemble something so broken? So completely and utterly demolished? How could she fix what she'd done?

He wanted her physically, but that was no longer enough for her. She wanted what she should have had in the first place. Roman, Ryan, a life together filled with love and happiness.

Was it possible? Would it *ever* be possible?

She could feel the change in him as they stood there in silence for too long, the slight stiffening of his body, the sudden urge to disconnect from her. She dropped her arms first, because she couldn't bear to cling to him and have him push her away.

He took a step back, his handsome face carefully blank, as if he'd erased every emotion. Caroline's world felt as if it had been turned inside out.

"You don't mean that, Caroline," he said, and she wondered for a moment what he was talking about. And then she remembered—she'd said she wished Sullivan's wasn't in her blood.

"What if I do?" Her heart felt as if it, too, had been turned inside out. She wondered if he could see everything she felt, as if the truth shone bright and hard from beneath the cracks in the veneer she'd been showing to the world for too long. "What if I want to go back and start again? Make a different choice this time?"

He didn't pretend not to know what she was talking about. She could see it in the rigid line of his jaw, the flashing of his blue eyes.

"Don't," he told her, his voice hard again. "You made your choice. Anything we might have had was destroyed when you walked away and took our child with you."

They had dinner on the veranda. Shrimp, jerk chicken, grilled vegetables, spicy rice and beans, and fried plantains. There was cool, crisp white wine, and coffee. Caroline ate in silence, listening to Ryan chatter about his day at the beach. Her gaze kept straying to Roman, who looked both uptight and relaxed at once.

He seemed to realize how critical it was to engage with Ryan when his son spoke to him. Though he appeared surprised by the continual questions being directed at him, he answered them admirably. Even confidently, as if he was beginning to understand that all he need do to be involved was make Ryan comfortable with him.

When the meal was over, Blake announced it was time for Ryan's bath. Ryan started to whine in protest.

"No arguments, young man," Blake said. "It's time."

Ryan turned to his mother. "I want Mr. Roman to go with me," he said, and her heart squeezed tight. Her gaze met Roman's over the table for the first time since he'd walked away from her that afternoon.

His eyes burned hot, searing into hers. She tore her gaze away, her heart skipping crazily. "You need to ask him," she told Ryan.

The boy turned to his father. She knew the effort it took for him to overcome his innate shyness. He was growing accustomed to Roman, that was clear, but they hadn't known each other very long yet. This request was a far bigger deal than perhaps Roman realized. She prayed that he would, however, and that he'd agree.

"Would you take me for my bath, Mr. Roman?" he asked, his little voice quieter than it had been, his eyes downcast.

For a painful heartbeat, Roman didn't speak. Then he met her gaze over Ryan's head, and while she wasn't certain what she saw there, she knew he understood the import.

Roman pushed back from the table and stood without a word. She almost held her breath, but she knew he was going to accept, knew that he was overcome by whatever chaotic emotions were whirling inside him, and that speech was beyond him at this second.

He held out his hand to Ryan. The little boy slipped from his chair and put his small hand in his father's much larger one. They stood that way for a moment, Roman looking hard at her. She couldn't tell what was behind that enigmatic stare—hatred? Rage? Resentment?

Probably some combination of them all. And then he looked away, and she felt bereft suddenly, as if she'd been standing in full sunlight and was then plunged into an arctic pool.

"You will have to tell me what this bath involves," Roman said, turning his full attention to Ryan. The two of them disappeared into the house, Ryan talking excitedly. They were gone for a handful of heartbeats before Caroline turned to look at Blake, her eyes shimmering with tears she couldn't hide.

"Oh, honey," Blake said, coming over and squeezing her shoulder. "It'll all work itself out. You'll see. He just needs time."

Caroline swallowed hard a few times before she could manage to speak. "I'm not sure it will. I ruined whatever he felt for me a long time ago."

Blake only smiled. "I doubt that, sweetie. I seriously do." He patted her shoulder before returning to his seat. "You'll see. Trust me."

Dear, sweet Blake. She laughed in spite of herself. "You're nearly as arrogant as he is, you know that?"

He looked smug as he speared a chunk of mango with his fork. "I know what I know."

Roman found her on the beach. He hadn't gone looking for her so much as he'd needed to get out and clear his head with a long walk in the tropical dusk. Apparently, she'd needed the same.

His heart twisted in his chest, as it often seemed to do these days, at the sight of her standing there with her golden hair streaming down her back, her shoes dangling from one hand, her long legs bare to midthigh, where the hem of her casual dress lay.

It hit him with a visceral punch to the gut just how much he hated her and wanted her.

Except he couldn't quite lie to himself anymore. He *didn't* hate her. He never had. He'd hated what she'd done to him, hated what her betrayal had cost him, but he didn't hate the woman. How could he? Especially now that he knew she was the mother of his child?

She'd been young and, he remembered, eager to please her father. Of course she would have done whatever Frank Sullivan asked her to do. Roman felt a bubble of anger well inside him at the thought of the man who'd cut him off so thoroughly. Yet even that didn't last long when he thought of the other man wasting away with illness.

He'd blamed the Sullivans for years for what had happened to his mother, but the truth was that his father had caused her condition. If Andrei Kazarov hadn't been a brute and a bully, she would have never needed the kind of care that had cost so much more than Roman could afford.

As he looked at Caroline now, he realized that what he felt for her was a giant tangle of things he'd never solve. It was like being caught in a labyrinth with a thousand possible threads to follow toward freedom. He suspected, however, that he was never getting free.

The waves broke close to shore tonight, and then rushed high up on the sand. Caroline stood with her back to him and let the water flood around her ankles before it rolled out to sea again.

He didn't make a sound, but somehow she heard him. She turned at his approach and stood there with the shoes dangling and one arm wrapped around her middle. Her eyes were huge in her pale face. For a minute, he wanted to go to her and drag her into his arms. But then he remembered his son calling him "Mr. Roman" and his heart throbbed with hurt.

She didn't say anything at all, just watched him with those eyes that held a world of pain, and he grew angry with himself for wanting to take that pain away. *He* was supposed to be the one in pain, not her.

He thought of his little boy tonight, of all the ways he'd felt so awkward and out of sorts, trying to help with a bath and bedtime. How could he ever forgive her for that?

"I'm sorry, Roman," she finally said. "For everything."

She made him feel rough inside, as if he'd been scraped against the rocks again and again.

"I don't believe apologies are enough."

She dropped her chin to her chest. "I know that. But it's all I have."

Roman moved closer, until he was standing beside her and gazing out to sea. She turned until they were both facing the same direction again. Neither of them spoke for the longest time. They simply listened to the waves crashing, crashing, crashing against the beach.

"When I went back to Russia, I had no money. I had no job." He swallowed, unable to believe what he was about to say to her. And yet he had to. He felt it in his bones. If he didn't let out the rage, he might never figure out how to move beyond it. "My mother had been in a nursing home. I sent money to care for her when I worked for your father. When I returned, I couldn't pay for her to stay there anymore."

Beside him, he could hear Caroline gasp. "Oh, Roman—"

He held up a hand to silence her. "*Nyet.* I had to move her into a cheap apartment in Moscow. My brothers and I took turns doing what we could. We hired a nurse to come as often as we could afford. Without the specialized care in the nursing home, she died sooner than we expected."

Fresh tears rolled down Caroline's face. He felt the guilt of it pierce him to the core. It wasn't her fault. If he'd kept working for the Sullivan Group, his mother still would have died. She just would have done so in a better environment.

"She was going to die, anyway," he said softly. "Her mind was already gone. Had been for years."

"What happened to her, Roman?"

He closed his eyes against the memories, the pain. "My father was a very violent man, *solnyshko*. We will leave it at that."

She closed the distance between them, wrapped her arms around his waist and held him tight, burying her head against his chest. For a moment he didn't move. And then, almost without thought, his arms went around her body and held her tight.

CHAPTER THIRTEEN

Rumblings of Leadership Changes at Sullivan's

CAROLINE FELT SO many things in that moment. Love, sadness, worry, sorrow, fear—and maybe a zillion other emotions she would never identify. "You never told me your mother was ill," she said against the warm hardness of his chest.

"We were too busy talking about other things," he said, his voice a rumble in her ear. "Whenever we did talk."

She pushed back to look up at him. There was sadness etched on his features. Pain. It made her heart ache. They had more in common than only a child, it would seem.

"I wish I'd known."

He shrugged. "There was nothing to be done. She was being taken care of."

Caroline squeezed his arms. "I'm so sorry. I understand what it's like to lose someone you love, and to feel utterly helpless to prevent it."

He pushed a lock of her hair that had blown free behind her ear. She shivered with the sensations that rolled through her at that simple gesture. "You were very much affected by Jon's death."

"He was my best friend." She pulled in a breath, determined to go on. "He was a good father to Ryan. He loved him as if Ryan were his own."

Roman didn't say anything for a long moment. "I am glad then. Since I could not be there."

Caroline swallowed. "You should have been. I should have found a way to tell you, once I knew where you were."

He blew out a breath. "I am beginning to think nothing is as simple as it seems, in retrospect. We both made mistakes."

Her breath caught. "Did we?"

He looked so serious. "*Da.* I believed you too readily when you told me you didn't love me. I should have fought harder."

"It wouldn't have mattered," she said, her throat aching with the weight of her words. "I still had to marry Jon in order to save the stores. I couldn't let people suffer when it was in my power to prevent it. And I couldn't see my heritage destroyed."

He took her hand in his, threaded his fingers

through hers. "And this is why you fight so hard now. Why you refuse to give up."

"It's Ryan's heritage, too. I can't let you break it up."

"He is my son, Caroline. He will inherit all I have built. If this includes Sullivan's, it will still go to Ryan."

Her heart skipped a beat. "I thought you wanted to demolish it."

He shrugged. "I am a business man, *solnyshko.* I will do what is best for the company, and for my bottom line."

So many feelings welled within her then—relief, love, gratitude. She'd thought he would destroy the stores simply to get back at her. She was used to her life falling apart just when she thought everything was going well.

But perhaps he wouldn't destroy anything. Perhaps they could build something good out of the ashes of the past. Perhaps, this time, it would all work out the way she wished.

"Sullivan's shouldn't be in this position," she said. "But it all went wrong when we didn't realize—" She swallowed hard. Her father's illness was something they'd kept from becoming public knowledge simply to prevent the media spectacle the news would bring.

"Didn't realize what, Caroline?"

Her chest ached. "We didn't realize that my father was in the beginning stages of Alzheimer's. That he was losing his sense of self, and had become easy prey to those who wanted to profit from his mistakes."

Roman looked stunned. "I can hardly believe it. Your father was always larger than life. Just five years ago…"

"I know. But it's true. He doesn't remember much of anything anymore. He doesn't know me at all. Or Ryan."

"*Solnyshko moya,* I'm sorry."

She looked away from him suddenly, fighting the tears that wanted to keep coming until there was nothing left, until she was an empty husk. Life was so different now than it had been five years ago. Two years ago.

Even one year ago.

It was lonelier and harder, and she was tired of it. Tired of putting on a brave face and pretending everything was okay. Tired of being strong when she felt anything but. When she wanted to howl and wail and gnash her teeth against the unfairness of it all.

"Caroline," he said, and she turned to look at him. "You don't have to be strong every moment of every day."

"I can't help it," she whispered. "It's all I know."

He cursed then, and dragged her against him.

She clung to him, to the warmth and hardness of his body in the tropical dusk. This was where she wanted to be. Where she'd always wanted to be.

In this man's arms, in his life. He was murmuring to her in Russian. She didn't know what he said, but it sounded beautiful to her ears.

And then he tilted her head back and fused his mouth to hers. It was a hot, wet, sensual kiss that sizzled into her like lightning. Her body was on fire. Needy.

His mouth slanted over hers, taking everything she gave him. They fell onto the wet sand as the sky turned purple and stars dotted the fabric of the night. His big body hovered over hers, pressing her into the surf.

When the tide rolled in again, she gasped with the rush of water over her body, but she didn't care that she was soaked. The sea was warm, but the breeze cooled her. Her nipples responded, beading tight against the thin cotton of her dress. Roman lifted himself away from her as she shuddered, concern in his gaze.

Whatever he might have said was lost, however, as his gaze slid over her. The dress clung to every curve, every dent and hollow of her body. His gaze fastened on her nipples. And then he was cursing softly, unbuttoning her dress and peeling it aside so he could fasten his warm mouth on her cold flesh.

Caroline arched her back, gasping when he curled his tongue around her nipple. This was what she wanted, what she'd missed for far too long. She'd had a taste of it that one glorious night they'd spent together in L.A., but it had been over so quickly.

Now, however, she reacted like a madwoman. Moaning and writhing and urging him onward. Before he changed his mind. Before something happened to break this magical spell between them.

She tilted her hips up, arching into him, glorying in the answering hardness pressing back into her.

"I want you," she gasped when he sucked hard

on her sensitive nipple, sending a spike of pleasure into her femininity. "Please, Roman."

He lifted his head then, and they stared at each other for several heartbeats. And then he dropped his head with a groan and kissed her. Caroline wrapped her arms around his neck, pulling her body into his as if she feared he would change his mind.

One hand slid down her form, over her hip, and then inward. He angled his body away to finish unbuttoning her dress before he peeled it open, revealing her to the night air and his hot eyes.

"Caroline," he said, his voice a growl against her skin. "How I want you."

Her heart soared at the need in his voice. This thing between them was like the tide—inevitable, relentless, timeless. It simply was, regardless of everything that should have killed it.

She trailed her fingers to the hem of his T-shirt. "Take me," she told him, her voice a choked whisper. "I'm yours."

With a growl, he took the shirt from her grasp and ripped it up and off his body. A moment later, her fingers were tangling with his as they both went for the ties to his board shorts. He made quick work of the thong beneath her dress, and then he was lifting her hips, his body finding hers and entering her with one long, hard plunge.

Their joining was intense, overwhelming, beautiful. They rose and fell like the tide, their bodies glorying in each other. Caroline reached the peak much too quickly, tumbling over the other side in a long, hard fall to the bottom. Roman followed her, his body stiffening suddenly, his hoarse cry echoing against the night and the whoosh of the waves.

She held him to her, suddenly afraid that he would leave before she'd even managed to pick up the pieces of her soul again. His breathing was harsh in her ear, as if he'd run a great distance. He rolled off her, but she clung to him as he turned, until they were both on their side, facing each other.

He lifted a hand, and then he was pushing her wet hair off her cheeks and throat, tucking it behind her ears. The gesture was unrelentingly tender, and her heart felt as if someone had put it in a vise. She ached with everything she felt, with everything she wanted to say, and yet she remained silent. Afraid.

"You slay me," he said softly. "In so many ways."

Her throat hurt. "I don't mean to."

"You have never meant to. And yet you do."

She slid her palm against his cheek. "I think it's mutual, Roman. I've never stopped thinking about you."

He captured her hand and pressed it to his mouth.

"I want you and our son in my life," he growled. "I want to figure this out, Caroline."

"We will," she said. "Somehow, we will."

Much later they lay in bed together, with nothing but the sound of the waves and bamboo wind chimes echoing in through the sliding doors that were open to the night. When they'd come inside from the beach, Caroline had almost expected to go their separate ways in spite of the way they'd clung to each other. This feeling between them was still so raw, so fragile, and she hadn't thought that Roman would want her in his bed.

But he'd had other ideas.

He'd tugged her toward his room, where they'd showered to remove the sand from their bodies, and then they'd fallen into the plush bed with the filmy mosquito net surrounding it and made soft, sweet love that tore her heart open and made it impossible to hide her feelings from him.

"I love you," she'd cried as she'd exploded beneath him. He hadn't said the words back, though her name had been on his lips as he'd followed her into oblivion.

Caroline couldn't sleep, so she climbed from the bed and went out onto the veranda, where she found a lounge chair and curled up in it. She was wearing one of Roman's T-shirts and she bent to inhale his scent from the fabric.

Then she lay back against the cushions and stared out at the whitecaps breaking against the shore. The moon was high now, its glow painting the sea with a glittery brush. She curled her toes into the chair and wrapped her arms around her body to ward off a chill.

"What are you doing out here?" Roman's voice was gravelly with sleep. She turned to him, her heart lurching at the sight of his bare chest—and barer thighs. He'd come outside in nothing but his own glorious skin, and she shivered anew—though not from cold.

"I couldn't sleep."

He sat on the lounge beside her and folded her

into his embrace. His body was warm and she snuggled closer to him, wrapping an arm around his torso.

"Do you wish to talk about it?"

She closed her eyes and pressed her lips to his skin. "There's nothing to talk about," she said.

He tipped her chin up and stared into her eyes. Her heart skipped as she imagined him loving her, really loving her, the way he once had. Was it possible? Would it *ever* be possible again? Or was she deluding herself, setting herself up for an even bigger fall?

"There must be something," he said, his voice low and deep and sexy.

She dropped her gaze from his. "I'm worried about a great many things, Roman. None of which I want to waste time talking about tonight."

"What do you wish to talk about then?"

She looked up again. His eyes were twin flames in the night and she shuddered at all she knew lay behind that enigmatic gaze. "What if I don't want to talk at all? What if I only want to feel?"

His smile curled her toes. "This can be arranged, *solnyshko*. But I'd prefer if you'd talk to me first."

She sighed. How could she ever voice everything she was feeling? "What's there to talk about, Roman? You already know everything."

His smile faltered, and her heart flipped. "Not everything, Caroline. In fact, I'd say I have missed much."

She squeezed him tight. She'd been talking about her father, about Sullivan's, but she knew what he meant without hearing him say it. Knew what that veil of sadness alluded to. "I have baby books, and videos. I know they aren't the same, but I want to show them to you when we get back to New York."

His gaze dropped, and she wanted to cry out. Everything was still so fragile between them that she kept expecting it to crack and fall apart. But he looked up again, his eyes glistening in the night. "Yes. I want to see these."

She turned her head away as tears pricked her own eyes. "I don't blame you for hating me."

He didn't say anything for a long moment. "I don't hate you, Caroline."

She looked at him, disbelief rumbling through her like a storm. "Why not? You lost a lot because of me. Because you got involved with me."

"I gained something, too," he said. "I gained a son."

She curled her fingers into a fist as hot emotion flooded her. "I'm angry with my father. Angry that he sent you away like he did, angry that he made poor decisions at Sullivan's, and angry that he doesn't even know me anymore—"

She broke off and bit down on her lower lip. Roman turned her chin toward him. "We cannot change the past. And for your father, we cannot change the future, either. But we can do something about *our* future."

Her breath caught. "Do you mean that?"

He looked so serious. "I do. Marry me, *lyubimaya moya*. Let us have the life we should have had together in the first place."

A week ago, she'd refused to consider marrying him. But so much had changed since then. Her feelings for him were raw, overwhelming. And it was so very tempting to agree this time.

But if she said yes, if she took this slice of happiness, would it last? Or would the fall to the bottom be even longer and harder than it had the first time?

"I'm scared, Roman. What if it doesn't work out?"

He sighed. "Then we will deal with that if the moment comes."

She shivered. That was something she didn't want to think about it. She pulled him down to her, until she was pressed full length to his amazing body. Until she could feel the heat and hardness of him, feel her blood stirring hot in her veins in answer.

"I don't want to talk anymore," she said, as dread threatened to crush the dreams she'd barely begun to have. "Kiss me, Roman."

His body responded, growing impossibly harder against her flesh. His breath hitched inward. "This conversation is not over, Caroline," he said, his lips only a whisper away.

She arched against him, desire a heavy drumbeat in her veins. Roman held himself still as the ocean washed against the beach and the bamboo chimes tinkled in the breeze—and then he cursed softly and took her mouth with his.

CHAPTER FOURTEEN

*Is Carol Pregnant? Rumors of an
Island Wedding...*

THE PRIMARY LESSON Roman had learned about love was that it didn't last. In his experience, it wasn't strong enough to overcome adversity. Yet here he lay, beside the woman he'd once loved more than the world, and his insides were twisted into knots at what he was feeling.

He'd held her in his arms and called her his love. Not that she knew what he'd said, but he did. The words—*lyubimaya moya*—had slipped out before he'd realized they were even there. Hovering like a tiger waiting to pounce, they'd caught him by surprise and torn shreds into his heart.

How could he mean them? How could he let himself be that vulnerable again?

How could he possibly love her?

He didn't know, but feared that he did. He also

feared, on some level, a repeat performance of five years ago. She'd said tonight she loved him—but did she mean it? Did she want him only in order to rescue her stores? Was that what this was all about?

He didn't know. But then he thought back on the last few days together, on the way she tried to ease his relationship with Ryan, and every instinct Roman had told him the answer was no.

Yet the questions swam in his head anyway. The past was like a serpent, coiled and waiting to strike.

Roman shoved a hand through his hair and forced out a breath. *Chert poberi,* this was supposed to be simple. His plan had been to return to New York and rip Sullivan's out from under the high and mighty Sullivan family. To make them pay for all the heartache they'd caused him.

Except he'd realized that wasn't the solution, no matter that he'd carried that very thought with him, let it drive him for years now.

Caroline had been as much a victim of the situation as he had. Her parents had forced her to leave him, and then forced him out of the country to prevent her from going back on her word.

As if she would. He looked down at her, curled beside him, and felt a pang of pride and desire. She was fierce and she did what she thought was right for those she loved. Even at the expense of herself. Would he have acted any differently than she had if faced with the destruction of so many lives?

He knew the answer was no. He would have done whatever it took. Just as she had.

He ran his fingers over the satin of her skin, smiled when she sighed and snuggled closer to him.

This felt right. Being with her. Being with Ryan. Roman wasn't betraying his mother's memory by giving up the idea of ruining Sullivan's. He knew she wouldn't have wanted him to do such a thing anyway. She'd been a gentle soul. Too gentle. It had been her greatest weakness and her ultimate destruction.

He grieved for her, but he couldn't blame anyone else for the consequences of her choices. He had to let it go. He had to move forward and embrace his future.

He turned on his side and tucked Caroline against his body, curving himself around her. She wriggled her hips against him and his body reacted, hardening instantly. She came awake—or perhaps she'd been awake—her hips moving more deliberately now, tormenting him.

"Are you planning to use that?" she asked almost breathlessly.

His mouth found the place where her neck joined her shoulder. "Would you like me to?"

In answer, she moved a leg forward, exposing her sex for him. He entered her from behind, filling her until they both gasped.

It was some time later when they collapsed into sleep, bodies curled around each other as if they feared being parted during the night.

Caroline sat in the office overlooking the beach and tried to focus on the phone calls she'd been making since 6:00 a.m. Outside, she could see Ryan playing on the sand. Blake sat in a chair beneath an umbrella, a cool drink beside him and a book in his hand.

She hadn't seen Roman since early this morning, when he'd woken her with kisses and caresses as the sun rose in the sky over the Caribbean. He'd told her he had business to take care of at the resort and that he'd be back later today. She glanced at her watch, realized it was after three in the afternoon, and wondered when he would return.

God, she was so pitiful, wanting him so much even as she worked harder than she'd ever worked in her life to keep her company from defaulting, and him from winning what he'd come to take away from her in the first place.

Not that she believed he would destroy Sullivan's now. No, she knew he was smart. He hadn't built a huge, multibillion dollar conglomerate out of nothing by being stupid. He would not demolish her stores just to satisfy a thirst for revenge if it wasn't smart business to do so.

Caroline sighed. She felt as if they were gaining an understanding of one another, as if the past was not so fearsome or unconquerable as she'd believed.

Oh, it still frightened her, definitely. She'd watched her life fall apart so many times in the last few years that it was hard to suppose it wouldn't again. Especially when happiness seemed to be within her grasp.

She closed her eyes a moment, swallowed. It would be all right. She firmly believed she and Roman could be reasonable and work through their issues like adults. They had a child together. If nothing else, they had to think of Ryan first.

Today, she honestly believed they could do that. A week ago, not so much.

Caroline set her cell phone on the desk. The spreadsheets open before her showed a better picture than they had just two weeks ago, but it wasn't enough. It wasn't going to *be* enough. She had to admit that now. She'd found investors, squeezed profits, but it simply wasn't enough to make the payment due.

They were going to default.

It hurt, but she had to accept the truth. Tomorrow, barring a miracle, Sullivan's would belong to Kazarov Industries. She still wasn't quite sure how she felt about that. Sad, scared, angry—a host of emotions boiled inside her at the thought of her family legacy passing into hands other than her own.

Her mother would be devastated. Her father wouldn't even know. Caroline watched Ryan upend a bucket of sand on the beach and Blake get up and go help him build a sand castle. She pushed back from the desk, determined to join them for a few moments in the hopes it would help her stress levels. Her phone rang before she reached the door.

She turned and went back to get it. It was her CFO. "What's up, Rob?"

"You aren't going to believe this," he said, his voice sounding as if someone had just told him he'd won the lottery, "but we have another investor. We've done it."

Her heart began to pound. "What are you telling me?"

"We'll have the money, Caroline. Kazarov won't win."

She sat back in her chair as her body went numb. "You're sure?" It didn't seem possible, and yet…

Sudden joy suffused her. But sadness followed hard on joy's heels. Which was stunning.

My God, she was actually sad that Roman was going to lose! She blinked at the incongruity of her feelings while Rob filled her in on their last minute savior.

"European investment group," he was saying. "Looking to expand their holdings in the States…"

The rest trailed into a buzzing in her ears as she tried to process everything. Sullivan's was going to continue. Under *her* leadership. Roman wasn't absorbing anything, breaking anything, selling anything.

She shook herself, forced herself to get her head back in the game, and began to grill Rob about the details. By the time the call was finished, she wanted to shout with joy. She wished that Roman was here so she could tell him.

How odd was that? The person she'd just defeated was the one person she most wanted to share this news with.

She shot up from her chair, her nerves suddenly on edge from the rush of adrenaline. Pacing, she punched in Roman's number and waited. He answered on the third ring.

"Roman," she said, when his beautiful voice filled her ears.

"Yes, my angel?" he replied, his voice full of warmth that tugged at her and made her want to wrap her arms around him.

She clutched the phone tight, wanting to say the words, but realizing she couldn't. She couldn't tell him like this. It had to be in person. "I was just wondering when you were returning."

"I'm on my way now," he said, and her limbs filled with delicious languor as she imagined their bodies entwined on silk sheets. "Is everything okay?"

"Never better," she said, though her heart pounded recklessly. "But hurry. I want you."

He chuckled softly and said something that made heat pool in her belly. Ten minutes later, she heard the slam of a car door, and she rushed to the front of the house. Roman came up the steps wearing a suit, which surprised her, since she didn't remember him leaving in a suit this morning. Then again, she'd been half-asleep when he'd left.

Her heart turned over with love for him as he swept her into his arms and kissed her thoroughly. Caroline wrapped her arms around his neck and arched her body into his. He made her feel gloriously alive when she'd been numb for so long.

Her nerves throbbed with tension in spite of her happiness. The last time she'd been so happy with him, everything went wrong.

She told herself there was no one here to force her to walk away this time. This time, she was in control. This time, for better or worse, it was *her* choice. And his.

She shuddered and ground her hips against him until she found what she sought.

Oh yes, he was ready for her.

"What has happened to put you in such a good mood?" he asked, kissing a trail down her neck before he took her hand and tugged her toward his room.

"I'll tell you later." She kicked the door shut behind her and turned him until he was against it. Her fingers went to his buttons, slipping them open expertly. "First, I have needs that require assuaging."

Roman laughed as she spread his shirt open and pressed her mouth to his golden skin. "Then I'm your man."

The tables turned quickly after that. He had her naked within moments. But instead of hauling her to the bed, he used the closest surface he could find, turning her until she was bent over the arm of the couch in the sitting area, her bottom high in the air, her body open to him.

He gripped her hips and slid into her while she arched her back and tried to get closer to him.

And then they were sailing into oblivion, his body hot and hard inside hers, playing her as if she were an instrument that only he knew. Caroline didn't last long. Within moments, she'd fallen over the edge of pleasure and tumbled deep into an orgasm that had her panting and gasping and begging him to make it last.

He did. And when it was done, when they were both spent, he tugged her into his arms and settled on the couch with her, brushing her hair off her damp forehead and pressing his lips to her skin.

"So tell me what put you in such a good mood, *solynshko.*"

Caroline's heart thumped. It was the moment she'd been waiting for, and now she wasn't certain what to say. Wasn't certain how he'd take the news.

Except if he took it badly, she'd know what that meant, wouldn't she? She'd know that everything between them had been false, and that he wasn't interested in her happiness so much as he was in winning. And as much as that prospect scared her, it was better to know it now rather than later.

She bit her lip and lowered her lashes. "We're making the payment," she said. "On time."

His laugh startled her and her gaze snapped to his. But he wasn't upset. This wasn't disbelieving laughter. Warmth spread through her blood, her bones. He seemed happy. Really, truly happy.

"Well done," he said, and then kissed her. "Sullivan's carries on, and the Sullivan heiress wins the day."

"You aren't upset?" she asked, even though it was a redundant question at this point.

His smile was brilliant, his blue eyes sparkling. "How could I be? I will get my money, and the hassle of making Sullivan's profitable still falls to you. It's win-win for me."

It hit her how perfect this moment was. They were naked on the couch, clothes strewn across the furniture and floors, and they were talking business. A bubble of happiness welled within her. This was what she wanted. A life with Roman. A life where she felt she was part of an equal partnership, where she was valued for her brain as much as her body or her pedigree. Her parents had had it wrong when they'd wanted to keep her from the business. Sullivan's *was* in her blood.

And so was Roman. She pushed away the tiny thread of panic that insisted on weaving through the fabric of her happiness. *It's fine. He's not upset. The bottom isn't going to fall out.*

"I was worried at how you would take the news," she said. "You seemed to want Sullivan's so badly."

He shrugged. "I can think of something else I

want even more." He bent and kissed her, softly, sweetly. Desire, so freshly sated, throbbed to life inside her again. "We should marry, Caroline. For Ryan. For us."

She sighed contentedly, stretching against him. *This.* This was what she should have had all along. This blissful, joyful, incandescent happiness. It was not going to fall apart. It was real, and true.

"We should," she said. "We definitely should."

He sat up and tugged her upright. "Get dressed. There's a priest at the resort."

Caroline laughed as she slid onto his lap and wrapped her legs around his waist. "We have time, Roman."

His body hardened, his shaft rising heavy and thick between them. "Perhaps we do, *lyubimaya moya,*" he said, his accent becoming more pronounced again.

Caroline purred in approval. "You *are* a man of many talents, Roman Kazarov."

They were married at sunset, on the beach where they'd made love. It was a private ceremony with only Blake, Ryan and the household staff for company. Caroline's head was still spinning from how quickly it had happened. Once they'd made love and gotten dressed again, Roman had asked her once more if she would marry him here, today, on this island.

Her heart filled with love, she'd said yes. Finally, she and Ryan and Roman would be a family.

She kissed Roman when the priest told her to, and then turned to find Blake watching with tears in his eyes. Ryan looked so serious in his little button-down shirt and shorts, and she laughed as he broke free from Blake and ran into her arms.

"It's okay, sweetheart," she told him as she bent to catch him and realized she was crying. "Mommy is very happy."

"Is Mr. Roman my daddy now?" he asked shyly, and Caroline tried not to break down with the happy, delirious tears that threatened.

"Yes, baby," she managed to reply. "That's right."

She picked him up and held him tightly against her. He turned wide eyes to Roman, who watched them both so carefully that it made her heart ache. He was still unsure with Ryan, though he was getting better. She smiled to encourage him and he smiled back, his grin breaking wide.

Her heart felt as if it would stop then and there.

Roman opened his arms, and she stepped into them. Ryan put his little arms around Roman's neck, and Roman laughed.

"I am happy to be your daddy," he said, and her heart squeezed tight.

They returned to the house and had a leisurely meal as a family, and then Blake took Ryan for his bath and bedtime. Caroline felt suddenly shy, which was ridiculous, when Roman came over and pulled her up from her seat.

"I want to make love to you," he said, his voice a soft growl that slid through her nerve endings and made her quiver with longing. "As my wife."

And then he picked her up and carried her to the bedroom, while she hid her face against his crisp white shirt. He kicked the door closed and undressed her slowly, thoroughly exploring her, as if he had all the time in the world. Even after she was naked, he took his time, tormenting her with his lips and tongue and teeth, before he finally sank deep inside her and took them both to paradise.

As her orgasm hit her, Caroline felt the words overwhelming her, rushing out of her as if they had to break free or choke her. "I love you, Roman!"

"Caroline," Roman said, holding her tightly. "My precious Caroline."

It was as close to an admission of love as he'd come, and she sighed happily before she fell asleep in his arms.

This time, it would work. Nothing would come between them ever again.

CHAPTER FIFTEEN

Kazarov Wins Again! But at What Price?

THE PHONE RANG in the middle of the night. Caroline turned over, coming awake slowly, while Roman talked to whoever had disturbed them, his voice hard and commanding even as he tried to keep it quiet.

She wished she understood Russian at that moment, because Roman did not sound happy. Another few minutes and he ended the call.

"What's wrong?" she asked, propping herself on an elbow beside him. He was sitting on the edge of the bed, raking his hands through his hair and yawning.

At the sound of her voice, he turned. "It's nothing," he said, tipping her chin up and kissing her softly. "Business."

"It didn't sound like nothing."

He sighed. "I have some things to take care of,"

he said shortly. "I need to return to New York. I'll be back in a day, maybe two."

Her heart fell into her toes. Two days seemed like a lifetime now. "I'll go with you," she said. "I have things to do at Sullivan's, anyway."

"This is our honeymoon, *angel moy*. You should not be working."

"Neither should you," she said, sitting up beside him and running her palms over the smooth muscle of his back.

"It cannot be helped," he said softly, turning and pushing her back onto the bed. His mouth found the hollow of her throat. "I'll be back before bedtime tonight, how's that?"

She sighed as her arms went around him. "It will have to do, I suppose. But Roman, maybe we should all go. There's too much going on right now—"

"Shh," he said. "You've won, *solnyshko*. The payment will be made on time, and you deserve a vacation after all your hard work. Worry about Sullivan's next week."

Caroline yawned and stretched. She was still so tired after a long day of phone calls, hot lovemaking and getting married. Still, she had every intention of dragging herself from the bed and going with Roman, but by the time she awoke again, he was long gone.

Caroline sat up in bed and blinked as the sun slanted through the blinds. Confusion clouded her brain, making everything fuzzy—and then she remembered last night and Roman's phone call.

Uneasiness pooled in her belly, though she didn't know why.

But she couldn't lie in bed any longer, so she showered and dressed and went to find Blake and Ryan. Blake was eating breakfast, while her son played with a toy car on the wide veranda. Beyond, the sea sparkled like diamond-tipped turquoise and the sun beat down on the white sand, though it was early yet.

Caroline sat at the table and reached for a piece of fruit. Blake was watching her, one corner of his mouth tilted up in a knowing grin.

"Stop looking at me like that," she said. "You are the nosiest nanny on the planet."

His grin got bigger. "I am. And I'm happy for you."

She was happy, too. Happy and even a little bit frightened. She had everything she wanted, but it had all happened so fast that her head was still spinning.

"Mrs. Kazarov," the housekeeper said, and Caroline turned toward the large woman in the colorful print dress, who held up a phone. "You left this in the office. It's been buzzing for twenty minutes at least."

"Thank you," Caroline replied, a bit chagrined as she took the phone. She'd forgotten that she'd left it plugged in last night when Roman had carried her to bed. She pressed the home button and her heart skipped a beat. There were missed calls, voice messages and even texts—both from her mother and from Rob.

That tiny feeling of panic she'd had earlier blossomed into a full-blown wave churning inside her.

With shaking fingers, she punched the first message and listened to it. She listened to three more, all some version of "Call me, there's a problem," until her nerves were wound so tight she shot up and went to the other end of the veranda to make a call.

Rob's voice came over the line. "Caroline, thank God."

"What's wrong?"

She could hear the strain in his voice when he spoke. "The Europeans are pulling out of the deal," he said, and her heart plummeted right through the wooden slats of the veranda. *Too good to be true.* She'd known it, hadn't she? Felt it keenly.

Rob sucked in a breath and she knew he was dragging on a cigarette. A habit he'd given up, she'd thought. Cold determination settled in her gut. Whatever was coming next, she had to deal with it.

"What else?" she said, bracing herself for it, knowing what was coming even as she did so.

"It's your father. The press—they know."

She'd been wrong. She couldn't prepare for that kind of blow. It wasn't quite the same as when the doctors had delivered the bad news to her and Jon that day. But it was still bad. Gut-wrenching in ways that made her feel so helpless and angry.

Her entire body went numb as she sank onto the nearest chair. She wanted to howl, and she wanted to throw things. Instead, she couldn't move. She'd been flattened. Around her, the world went on as before. But everything had changed.

Again.

* * *

Getting off the island was not simple, especially when she had to book a private charter just to get to Miami. Blake was tight-lipped beside her, while Ryan complained about having to sit still instead of run and play as he had on Roman's plane.

Caroline sat with her arms folded and her head turned to stare out the window. She was completely numb. And furious with herself.

She thought back over the hours since that first phone call. Her initial thought had been to call Roman and ask for his help. But then Rob had told her that representatives from Kazarov Industries had arrived to oversee the transfer of Sullivan's, and her belly had turned to ice.

Roman had gotten a phone call in the middle of the night. And he'd told her to stay on the island, that she wasn't needed, that Sullivan's was safe. So he could steal it out from under her?

She'd refused to let herself think such a thing, though her soul had gone numb at the mere idea. After she'd hung up with Rob, she'd tried to call Roman, her fingers shaking as she punched in the number. He hadn't answered. Not entirely unexpected, since he could be in a meeting.

So she'd tried again. And again.

Then she'd left messages—countless messages.

He did not return her call. For hours, she didn't hear a word.

Finally, as the day dragged on and she heard nothing from the man she'd married, she'd had to accept the truth. Just as she'd had to accept the truth when her father had told her she needed to marry Jon to save the stores, or when Jon's doctor had told her the chemo wasn't working and he was dying, or when her father had ceased to be the vibrant, brilliant man he'd always been and become a confused, frightened individual.

The truth hurt. She hated the truth. She didn't want to believe it.

But one thing she'd learned in the last five years was that denying the truth didn't make anything better. Just like ripping a Band-Aid from her skin, it was better to do it quickly. Better to accept the cold, hard, terrible truth than to pretend it wasn't happening.

And the truth was that Roman had betrayed her. He hadn't given up his notion of revenge at all. Why would he? She'd broken his heart, taken his child from him. Her father had cost him his livelihood and his ability to take care of his dying mother. That was an awful lot to forgive in such a short time.

He hated the Sullivans, regardless that he might want her physically or that he wanted their child. The truth of that statement was like a dagger to her heart.

Had he told her he loved her? No. He'd made no promises that he ever would. She'd let her heart fill in the blanks, had let herself believe what she wanted so desperately to believe: that it was possible.

Instead, he'd taken her information, her good news, and worked to thwart it. What other explanation could there be?

Worse, he'd leaked information about her father. He'd had to know news of that sort would scare her investors in the interim. That hurt most of all.

She'd called her mother, who was holding up well, though she'd had to barricade herself and her husband in the house in order to prevent prying photographers with telephoto lenses from capturing pictures. The story of Frank Sullivan's Alzheimer's was big news, and a current image of him looking vacant-eyed or gaunt would only serve to increase circulation of that day's paper.

Caroline despised the vultures. But she despised herself even more. How could she be so gullible? So blind and stupid? How could she have let Roman into her life the way she had, knowing what he'd wanted from her in the first place? He'd never pretended to want anything different, except at the end. And she'd stupidly believed him. Stupidly trusted him.

Now she was married to him. He'd made sure of that before he'd left, hadn't he? He'd made sure, so she couldn't take Ryan from him once he'd snatched Sullivan's out from under her. She remembered him telling her to relax, telling her she'd won, telling her to stay on the island and enjoy herself.

She'd relaxed her guard, and he'd brought the knife across her throat while she wasn't looking.

Sullivan's had defaulted at noon, eastern daylight savings time. She imagined Roman striding into the corporate office, his minions in tow. How smug he must be. How utterly gleeful.

It was nearly nightfall when Caroline's small entourage finally landed at JFK. Blake flagged a taxi. Once she got him and Ryan home again, she instructed the driver to take her to the Sullivan Group headquarters. The store was still open, its shining storefront gleaming in the darkness. She walked inside and let the familiar scents wash over her. Everything smelled new, clean, luxurious. It reminded her of home, because it had always been a home to her.

And now it was no longer hers. Or Ryan's.

Caroline went to the administrative area and took the private elevator up to the corporate offices. The workday was over for the business staff, but a few desk lights remained on as people continued to work well after quitting time.

Caroline stopped to stare at the stylized *S* of the logo etched into the glass doors. What would it become in the future?

She marched toward her office—to do what, she didn't know. Roman looked up from behind her desk when she walked in, and she saw red. Of everything she'd expected, that hadn't even made the top ten. It was a shock to see him. And it hurt far more than she'd ever thought possible.

"Couldn't wait to move in, I see," she said bitterly.

He stood, his handsome face creased in a frown. "Caroline, what are you doing here?"

She knew she had to look like hell after all the travel, but she didn't care. She tugged at her sundress, trying to remove the wrinkles, and lifted her chin to stare him directly in the eye. For the barest of moments, she wanted to rush into his arms. Wanted him to hold her and tell her it was all a mistake.

Better to rip the bandage off quick.

"Did you think I would stay on the island once I found out what you were doing?"

He didn't say anything for a long moment. His expression grew dark. "And what is it you think I am doing?" he asked, his voice containing a hint of danger that slid over her nerve endings and made the hair on her neck stand up.

She ignored the question. "My father," she said finally, fighting for control over her emotions so she wouldn't break down and sob. "How could you tell them about my father?"

He looked thunderstruck. "You are accusing me of telling the press about your father's illness?"

"Who else?" she demanded, wrapping her arms

around herself to ward off a sudden chill. "Who else stood to gain from it?"

She'd asked herself that question for hours now, and there was only one answer.

He came around the desk, his powerful form lethal and dark with suppressed energy. His face was a study in controlled rage. "How many people knew about your father?"

His voice was a whip in the quiet office, and she recoiled from the potency of it. But only for a moment. Her strength surged back, along with her anger, and she took a step toward him.

"There were a few, but none of them would tell."

"No health care workers, no gardeners at the estate, no secretaries or delivery people? My, how fortunate you are to control so much."

His words stung. And made her furious. "It has never been an issue until now. You are the one with the most to gain."

His eyebrows shot up. "Gain? You think I have something to gain by informing the press that my wife's father is a tragically sick man?"

Wife. How that word hurt. She shoved it aside and spread her arms wide. "This. You had all of this to gain. Is it any coincidence that my new investors decided to back out on the very same day my father's illness was leaked to the press? I may be the CEO in truth, but there are still those who believe my father is the power behind the throne."

Roman appeared ashen for just a moment—or maybe it was her imagination, because he suddenly looked very, very angry. "You believe I would do this. You truly believe it."

"Am I wrong?" she demanded. Part of her wanted him to deny it. Part of her wanted to believe those denials. But the evidence was overwhelming. They'd known each other such a short interval this time. How could she truly know what Roman Kazarov would do when he'd had five years to hate and plan?

"What do you think?" he asked, turning it back on her. A muscle ticked in his jaw. A very fine, very tiny muscle that hinted at how close he skated to the edge of control.

"I think you came to New York with a plan," she said, her stomach twisting and churning with hurt and anger and sadness. "And I believe you were willing to do whatever it took to see that plan through."

"I see," he said tightly.

Her breath hitched in suddenly, and she worked to control it. If he'd stabbed her through the heart with the letter opener lying on her desk, it couldn't have hurt worse. "You aren't denying anything."

He shoved his hands in his pockets. For the first time, she noted that he looked a bit disheveled. His jacket and tie were gone, thrown over a chair, and his hair was mussed. His eyes, she noted, were bloodshot.

She felt a pang of sympathy, but she hardened her heart against it. She would never feel sympathetic to him again. He probably looked haggard because he was working so hard to enjoy his triumph. No doubt he was already fielding offers for the real estate sitting beneath her stores, and counting his money gleefully.

"Why should I?" he said in answer to her accusation. "You have already made up your mind."

How did he make her feel badly, when he was the one in her store? In her office? He held the smoking gun, and yet she felt as if someone had fed her a glass omelet. Her stomach was torn to shreds, along with her nerves.

She felt so tired all of a sudden. Drained, and

not because of the long day of travel. "Why are you here?"

He shrugged. "You defaulted today. I am here to claim my prize." His voice was so cold, so hard. He wasn't the man she'd made love with last night. The man she'd stood on the beach with, the one who'd opened his arms and held both her and Ryan close, as if he cherished them. She felt as if she would be physically ill.

"I don't know why you're angry," she said, her throat aching as she forced the words out. "I called you a dozen times. I left messages. You never replied. And now you are here, in *my* office, with my company arrayed before you. How could there possibly be any other explanation except the one that seems so obvious to us both?"

He turned and went back to the chair, sank down on it. His eyes glittered with heat and unspoken anger. Such deep, deep anger. She shivered—and refused to feel anything other than anger of her own.

"There isn't, of course. Because you know everything, Caroline."

Her eyes filled with tears. One spilled down her cheek. Her heart was breaking in two and he didn't care. "I loved you, you idiot," she said. And then she laughed. "Or maybe I'm the one who's an idiot. An idiot for believing in you."

His hands were fists on the desk. *Her* desk. His eyes were bleak, harsh. "Yes, some belief. It lasted all of a few days, I think."

She felt a pinprick of guilt—and that angered her. "How dare you try to turn this around on me? I denied it when Rob told me your people were coming to oversee the transfer, and I denied all day that you would do this to me, until it was obvious you weren't going to call me back and tell me I was wrong."

"So long? I am impressed."

He sounded cold, and it hurt that he could after they'd been so hot together only hours before. Caroline closed her eyes, searching for strength. She just wanted it all to go away. She wanted to rewind the clock and have this go much differently.

"You've won, Roman. Congratulations."

He stood again and she took a step backward. Then she whirled and strode from her office as regally as she could manage. She made it to the elevator without him stopping her, and jumped behind the doors just as they started closed. She absolutely refused to break down until she was safely on her way to the ground floor.

But even then, she was too numb to do so.

He was an ass. An incredible, stupid ass for allowing that to happen. Roman sank onto the chair and watched her go, his pride too wounded for him to follow as he should.

What was the matter with him? He raked a hand through his hair and slumped in his chair. *Her* chair.

He knew it looked bad, and yet he'd foolishly thought something fundamental had changed between them on the island. That she would believe in him because she loved him, and that she would wait for him to explain what was going on.

Instead, she'd jumped to every rotten conclusion she could in the space of a few minutes. He told himself that he should have expected it, but foolishly he'd anticipated a different reaction from her.

She'd said she loved him. She'd said she wanted to be a family. He'd thought that meant something. But instead of choosing him, choosing to believe in him, she'd chosen her family—the Sullivan family—once again. If something bad was happening to the Sullivans, and Roman Kazarov was around, then he must be the one to blame.

Roman blew out a breath. He'd never expected her to leave the island and come here. He should have. He should have expected exactly that, because Caroline was too stubborn, too driven, to ever sit quietly while something was happening to her precious company.

She believed the worst of him. She believed that he'd married her, made love to her, claimed her as his again and again, with the sole intention of duping her out of her legacy.

Once, he might have done so. Once, before he'd realized he still loved her. That he'd always loved her, and that she was his soul mate. Not that he'd ever believed in such ridiculous crap, but he knew it was true with Caroline. She was the only woman he'd ever loved, the only one he'd ever felt this inexplicable kinship with. Even now, in spite of the hurt and rage, he wanted her.

But she did not want him. That thought made the breath seize in his chest. Could that truly happen? Could she deny him?

A chill skated over him then. She could. She had done so before.

His inner beast wanted to smash things, but he refused to let it out. He still had work to do, papers to sign, and then he would go home and collapse on his couch with a shot of vodka.

Alone. The thought made him want to howl.

Go after her. Go now.

Roman shook his head to rid himself of the voice. He had to give her time to think, time to cool down. And he had to give himself time to cool down, too.

Because he was murderously angry, and that was no way to feel when he faced Caroline again. There was too much at stake, too many hurtful things that could be said. He wanted to face her rationally, calmly.

And then he wanted to drag her into his arms and never let her go. Except, he acknowledged, he might very well have to.

CHAPTER SIXTEEN

A Happy Ending for Caro and Kazarov,
After All?

THIS WAS NOT how she'd thought it would end for her and Sullivan's. Caroline sat on the couch in her living room, staring at the television, though she wasn't really paying attention to what was on. It had been two days since she'd left Sullivan's, and she was still thinking about Roman, about the way he'd looked at her when she'd walked in and accused him of stealing her company out from under her.

He'd looked…disappointed. And hurt.

Or maybe that was just wishful thinking.

She couldn't stop thinking about him, about the way she'd lain in his arms their last night together, the way she said she'd loved him when he made her climax for the zillionth time. She couldn't stop thinking about how he made her feel, or how he held Ryan's little hand and went wherever their son wanted to tug him.

Roman had seemed happy on the island. Happy with them.

But, clearly, not happy enough to put a stopper in his thirst for revenge.

She'd been deluded into thinking so. Whenever she thought about his reaction when she'd told him about her new investors, it made her heart hurt. The truth was that she'd seen what she wanted to see instead of what was really behind the curtain.

And she should have known better. Life had dealt her almost nothing but heartache for five long years. Why would it suddenly hand her everything she wanted right when she most wanted it? It was simply another way of reminding her how fragile happiness was, how fleeting.

"Are you planning to sit there all day again?"

Caroline turned to look over her shoulder at Blake. He was dressed in shorts and a Willie Nelson T-shirt that would have made her laugh if she hadn't been so sad. He was holding a backpack and his sunglasses were perched on his head.

"Are you going to the park?" she asked.

"We are, just as soon as Ryan figures out which toys he wants to take. Do you want to come?"

Caroline shook her head, her long ponytail brushing her neck, reminding her that she hadn't gotten dressed since she'd come home the other night. She'd sat in her pajamas day after day, watching television.

Ryan came running down the hall then, chattering happily about the robot he was taking with him to the park. He ran to her side. "Mommy, do you want to come play with me and Uncle Blake? We're going to have ice cream, too."

Caroline ruffled her son's hair. He was so like Roman that it hurt to look at him. "Mommy's going to stay home today," she said. "But you have fun."

Ryan's face screwed up in a frown. "Where is Mr. Roman? I mean Daddy," he corrected, and her heart felt ripped in two. "I want to show him my robot."

Caroline sniffed. "He's working, sweetie, but he'll be back soon."

Blake was frowning at her, but what else could she say? She and Roman were still married, and for Ryan's sake, they were going to have to figure out what came next. He would always be a part of Ryan's life, even if he wasn't a part of hers.

The thought of him not being in her life made a fresh wave of tears press against the backs of her eyes. *Stupid.*

Ryan and Blake left after a few more minutes of making sure they had everything they needed, and then Caroline called her mother. She'd been checking in every few hours, just to see how her mom was faring. Surprisingly, after the initial shock of her father's diagnosis reaching the press, the coverage had leveled off quickly. There were a few photographers lurking outside the estate, but most of them had gone. The stories in the papers were thoughtful and serious now. The more Caroline read, the more she began to think of ways in which she could support Alzheimer's research.

There would be no cure for her father, but maybe one day others could be helped. It was a thought that buoyed her up during the conversation with her mother.

When Caroline finished the call, the house was quiet. Too quiet.

She had to get up. She had to stop moping, and figure out what to do next. She wasn't a quitter and she despised sitting around and feeling sorry for herself. That ended here and now.

After a quick shower, she tugged on jeans and a silk tee with sandals. Then she pinned her hair onto her head in a messy bun and swiped on lip gloss and mascara. She was presentable, at least. She grabbed her purse as she swept through the kitchen. Maybe she'd walk over to Milk & Cookies Bakery and get some of their fabulous homemade cookies, then go to the park and surprise Blake and Ryan.

Ryan loved chocolate chip.

Plan made, Caroline yanked open the front door—and came to a screeching halt at the sight of the man with gorgeous blue eyes staring up at her from the bottom step. She clutched the door as her heart throbbed.

"What do you want?"

Something flickered in his eyes, but then it was gone. Annoyance? Anger? Fear?

"I want to talk to you."

She swallowed. "Fine, say what you need to say and go."

One eyebrow lifted. "There is a man across the street in a blue sedan. He is a photographer, and his lens has been pointed at us since you opened the door. Do you really wish to do this here?"

She waited for the space of several heartbeats, her fingers pressing hard against the mahogany of her door. And then she stepped back and swung it open in silent invitation. Roman came up the steps and into her house. She shut the door behind him, shrinking back as he turned to face her.

The look on his face was a mixture of anguish and rage. She'd let a lion into her den and now she would pay the price.

"I have been thinking very hard, Caroline," he began, his voice as cool as silk. "And no matter how I try, my anger refuses to abate."

Shock rooted her to the spot, but only for a moment. "Your anger? *Your* anger? I'm not the one who deceived you."

"Ah, but you did," he said, his eyes flashing hotly. He took up all the space in her foyer, though it was huge. He took all the space because his presence was that big. And because he had been central to her life almost from the moment she'd met him.

He took a step closer and she ducked toward the living room, putting a couch between them. She didn't know why, but it seemed the safest course.

"I have no idea what you mean, Roman. You're talking nonsense."

"Am I? You said you loved me, Caroline. You lied."

"How dare you—"

"I dare because it is true. If you loved me, you would not believe such bad things about me. If you loved me, you would give me a chance to explain without accusing me of ruining your life."

"I did give you a chance!" she yelled. "I called and called you that day!"

For the barest moment, he looked chagrined. But then his anger was back, full force. "If you had trusted me, you would have learned the truth in good time."

"How dare you come here and say that to me?" she whispered. How dare he stand there, looking so much bigger than life, and tempt her with what she wanted most in this world—for everything to work out, for it to have all been a mistake.

Life didn't work that way.

Or it didn't for her. It never had.

Without a word, he took a folded packet of papers from his back pocket and tossed it at her. At

first, she only stared at it, lying on the floor between them.

"What is that?"

"Pick it up."

It seemed to take an age, as if she were afraid
of what she'd find, but she finally bent and re-
trieved the thick envelope, smoothing it where it
had been folded. She clutched it to her chest and
stared at him.

"Open it, Caroline."

She did as he said, her heart suddenly throbbing
hot and quick. And then it stopped beating and she
felt the color drain from her face.

Roman took an alarmed step toward her, but she
put her hand out and steadied herself on the back
of the couch. Confusion swirled inside her. "You
don't own Sullivan's."

His nostrils flared. "*Nyet,* this is true."

"But I thought…"

"I know what you thought," he snapped. "You
were wrong."

Her stomach twisted. "Why didn't you tell me
before?"

"You mean when you walked in and accused me

of seducing you, lying to you and stealing your heritage?"

She nodded, a lump forming in her throat.

He shoved a hand through his hair. Roman was always so cool, so controlled, and yet he looked as if he hadn't slept much in the past two days. His dark hair stood up in places. His eyes were red, as if he'd been drinking, and there were shadows under them.

"I should have," he muttered. "But I was stunned. And angry. I did not react well." He met her gaze evenly. "Besides, when you walked in, I technically did own Sullivan's. I was working to undo that."

She came around and sank down on the couch, her legs unable to hold her any longer. She could hardly believe what she was hearing. Hope was an insistent spark inside her, though she cautioned it not to grow just yet. "Why didn't you return my calls?"

"I regret that," he said softly. "But I was in meetings when you first called. By the time I knew you'd heard the Europeans had pulled out, I was working hard to fix it. They'd heard about your father and got cold feet. I was trying to talk them into investing anyway, because I wanted to give you good news when I called. I did not expect you to walk into the office."

"I wish you had just told me," she said, her heart beating double time. If he'd told her, she wouldn't have been so scared. And she wouldn't have made a fool of herself.

Or would she?

"And what would you have done, Caroline? Would you have stayed on the island and waited for me, or would you have done exactly the same thing and come running back to New York?"

She swallowed. They both knew the answer. "I wouldn't have stayed."

"Yes. This is why I did not tell you."

She sat there and stared at the papers in her hand. He'd really given her back her company. They'd defaulted, but he'd worked to undo it all. And he'd handed it back with generous conditions. Sullivan's would once again thrive, thanks to him.

A new thought occurred to her then. She remembered him on the island in his suit. He'd left early and returned after a long day away. "You were the one who found the last minute investor, weren't you?"

She'd been on the phone for days, working hard to find the money, and then someone she hadn't even talked to miraculously invested at the last minute?

Roman's gaze was steady. *"Da."*

"That same day I told you," she said. "That's why you were gone all day."

He nodded. "The chairman of a very large financial firm is a guest at the resort. I went to meet with him."

Tears filled her eyes then. "Why would you do that?"

"Because I wanted you to win." The words were simple, stark. And if she hadn't been sitting, they would have knocked her over.

Yet it was still so hard to believe. When she believed, when she let go and thought that good things were going to happen to her, life knocked her flat on her behind. "Not too long ago, you wanted me to lose. You wanted to punish me."

"Things changed."

She found herself leaning forward. Maybe she should be angry that he'd interfered, instead of letting her succeed or fail on her own, but she found she was far more riveted by what had motivated him. "What changed, Roman?"

He closed his eyes, and her heart felt as if it would stop beating in the next few seconds. She realized then that it all came down to this moment. It was as if her entire life depended on his next words.

"I realized that I love you, Caroline. That life without you is too stark, too lonely. That I would rather see you happy than sad, and that I'd lose a hundred companies if it made you so."

She bowed her head, joy suffusing her even as a terrible feeling of dread rose inside her soul. Once more, she'd made a horrible mess of things. And, once more, how could she be certain this was real? That tomorrow wouldn't ruin everything?

"How can you possibly love me after what I said to you? After I accused you of such terrible deeds?"

She heard him sigh. "I'm still angry with you. But love doesn't stop because someone hurts you. If it does, then it's not love, is it?"

Tears fell freely down her cheeks now. She dropped the papers and stood, facing him across the room. She wanted to go to him, but was scared to do so.

"I'm sorry, Roman. I should have given you a chance. But I was just so miserable, because I love you so much and I couldn't bear the thought that you didn't love me. And then, when the news of my father came out, I thought the worst...."

His face was stark with emotion. "It seemed easier to believe I would hurt you than that I might help you because I loved you?"

She nodded, and a hot tear fell on the back of her hand. God, she was a mess. An emotional, quaking mess. "That's what happens in my life, Roman. I've lost so many people I love. You. Jon. My father." She choked back the lump in her throat. "I thought I was losing you again."

"Caroline," he said softly. And then he opened his arms. She rushed into them, squeezing him tight. "I'm sorry, *lyubimaya moya,*" he said, his lips against her hair. "I should have told you how I felt. I should have told you what I was doing. You aren't losing me."

She buried her face against the hard plane of his chest. "How can you say that, when it's my fault? I should have given you a chance to explain. I should have known you wouldn't do such a terrible thing—"

He tilted her chin up and kissed her swiftly. She melted into his embrace, her entire body trembling with adrenaline and desire.

"We have both made mistakes," he admitted hoarsley. "Neither of us is perfect."

She laughed, the sound broken. "You could have just extended the loan in the first place, you know. That would have worked, too."

His smile was gentle. "Yes, but I wanted you to win. It seemed important to you."

"Not as important as you," she said honestly, and he squeezed her tighter. "I've longed for you every day for five years, even when I tried to pretend I didn't. If I lost Sullivan's, I wouldn't care, so long as I still had you. When I walked into my office the other night, I thought I'd lost you both. And losing you was the more frightening of the two."

He shuddered, his big body rippling from head to toe. "You didn't lose me. I love you, Caroline. And I love our son. I lost five years with you. I don't want to lose another minute."

Caroline swiped her fingers over her eyes. "I

don't know why you love me after everything that's happened, but I'm glad you do."

He sank onto the chair behind him and pulled her down with him until she was sitting across his lap. Then he stroked a finger over her cheek, her lips, while she shivered and ached and realized how very much she wanted him in that moment.

"I love you because I can do nothing else. I've loved you, since the first moment I saw you so many years ago. You're strong, Caroline, and fierce. You've put yourself and your needs last while you took care of others, and you've sacrificed so much. How could I help but love someone so brave that she would do that for other people?" He kissed her cheeks, her nose. "But even were you not so brave, I would love you. You are hardwired into my DNA. I could as soon breathe underwater as I could cut you from my life. It's not possible to live without you."

Caroline put her palms on either side of his face, smiling through her tears. Her heart was full of joy for the first time in a very long time. True, real joy that she no longer feared would be snatched from her tomorrow.

"You're an amazing man. And I think you'd better take me to the bedroom now. I have much to apologize for."

"No more apologizing," he told her, his handsome face serious. "We have too much living to do."

Caroline laughed tearfully. "Then take me to bed, Roman. I have much living I want to do. *Urgent* living."

Roman kissed her until she was dizzy with need. And then he stood, still holding her, and strode toward the stairs. "I think we'd better find that bed, *solnyshko*. I have some living of my own I'd like to try...."

EPILOGUE

*Sullivan's Posts Huge Gains on
Leadership of Chief Executive Officer
Caroline Sullivan Kazarov*

*Expecting for Real! Caro Glowing,
Kazarov Beaming*

*Scandalous Kazarovs Spend One-Year
Anniversary in Restaurant,
Entirely Absorbed in Each Other*

CAROLINE THUMBED THROUGH the newspapers that Blake had saved, laughing at the ridiculousness of some of them. He did it to tease her, she knew, but she truly enjoyed them. Or she did these days, anyway.

She hadn't enjoyed them at all when her father had been so prominently featured, but Roman had tracked down the source of that story. A home health care aide that her mother had fired for petty thievery had been behind the leak. The man had thought he could make a quick buck. And he had, but then he'd lost it all by gambling it away at a casino in Atlantic City.

Divine justice, perhaps. Caroline had no sympathy for anyone who thought he was entitled to profit from someone else's misfortune.

She put her hand on her stomach as the baby kicked. Roman walked in just then and found her grimacing.

"What is the matter, *solnyshko?* Is everything all right?"

"Fine," she said. "But I think this little girl is going to be a kickboxer."

"She gets it from your side of the family," he said, and she turned to gape at him.

"I beg your pardon?"

Roman laughed as he came over and sat down beside her on the veranda of their Caribbean getaway.

"You are a fighter, Caroline. I've never known anyone who fought harder for what she wanted than you have."

"Except maybe you."

He laughed again. "All right, so I fight too. Perhaps she gets it from us both."

"Then she will be formidable."

"Like her mother."

Caroline frowned. "I'm not feeling so formidable these days. I feel fat and hungry."

"You are gorgeous, my love. Would you like me to get you something from the kitchen? I believe there is some jerk chicken in the fridge."

"Mmm, that sounds good," she said. But then she held up her hand. "No, I'm not doing it. Fruit, that would be better. I'll take a banana. And some mango."

"As you wish."

Caroline watched her husband walk away, her heart swelling with so much love and happiness. They'd been married for over a year now, but she still felt as if they were on their honeymoon.

The only sadness in her life was the continuing deterioration of her father's condition, but she'd instituted a campaign in the stores where the profits from a particular line of merchandise went into Alzheimer's research. One day, maybe, there'd be a cure for those afflicted. It wouldn't come in time to help her father, of course. He was now in an assisted living facility, and her mother was learning to live life alone.

Roman returned with her fruit. "Your mother called me today," he said, as if he'd known Caroline had been thinking about her parents. He laughed at her disbelieving look. "Yes, she called *me*. I believe she's coming around. She might even like me now."

Caroline smiled up at him. "You do have a way with the ladies, Roman. I think it's the sexy Russian accent."

He winked at her. "Perhaps. Anyway, she wished to know if you were getting enough rest and taking your vitamins. I told her you were."

Caroline shook her head. "I think she wanted an excuse to talk to you. She could have asked me those questions. Did she say anything else?"

"Not really. She is planning a visit. That's about it." He shrugged. And then he nodded at the tablet Caroline was holding, and the email visible there. "How is Blake these days?"

"He's painting again," she said happily. "And he's dating. I'm pleased for him. But I miss him, too."

"I know you do. But it's good he's reentering life. It takes time when you lose someone you love,"

Roman said. And then he frowned. "Though I have yet to forgive him for making me hire a new nanny. This one is nowhere near as fun."

"She's a bit older than Blake," Caroline said, laughing. "Mrs. Steele isn't going to take Ryan surfing, or run down the beach with him. But she will be fabulous when little Claire wakes up in the middle of the night for the tenth night in a row, mark my words."

Roman shrugged. "As you say, my love." He settled against the cushions and took the papers from her that Blake had sent. "I would call these trash," he said after a few moments, "but damn if they don't seem to be true. We *are* ridiculously happy, are we not?"

"We definitely are."

He put the papers down and reached for her hand. They sat beside each other, watching the waves roll into shore, until Ryan came running up the steps from the beach and dumped a load of shells at their feet. Then they oohed and aahed appropriately, while their son talked a mile a minute about each and every one.

* * * * *

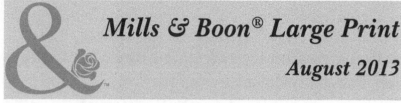

Mills & Boon® Large Print
August 2013

MASTER OF HER VIRTUE
Miranda Lee

THE COST OF HER INNOCENCE
Jacqueline Baird

A TASTE OF THE FORBIDDEN
Carole Mortimer

COUNT VALIERI'S PRISONER
Sara Craven

THE MERCILESS TRAVIS WILDE
Sandra Marton

A GAME WITH ONE WINNER
Lynn Raye Harris

HEIR TO A DESERT LEGACY
Maisey Yates

SPARKS FLY WITH THE BILLIONAIRE
Marion Lennox

A DADDY FOR HER SONS
Raye Morgan

ALONG CAME TWINS...
Rebecca Winters

AN ACCIDENTAL FAMILY
Ami Weaver

0713 Rom LP